Praise for *Four Christmas Kisses:*

"A snowed-in manor house, a mysterious stranger who's not what he appears and a delightful heroine torn between temptation and duty. This delicious story has a huge dollop of Christmas coziness and a strong current of sizzling passion. Highly recommended and guaranteed to get you into the festive spirit!" ***Annie West,* USA Today bestselling author**

"Oh, this was joyous! I think *Four Christmas Kisses* is one of my favorite Anna Campbell Christmas stories. It is full of Christmassy loveliness with lots of snow and festive spirit, a charming romance and gorgeous characters. I particularly loved Winifred and the murderous Edwina, and heroine and hero Anthea and Christopher were lovely. Very, very satisfying." ***Cathryn Hein, bestselling author of* The Country Girl**

"Anna Campbell never disappoints, her words always take me on a magical journey back in time to Ladies and Gentlemen who know how to fall in love and this one is no exception, I loved meeting Anthea and Christopher and of course Anthea's sisters, a beautiful Christmas story that left me smiling." ***5 stars, Romance Book Haven***

"The book has lies, heated kisses, great secondary characters, lots of mistletoe, some laughs, some tears, and of course a HEA complete with an epilogue. This is the fourth book in the series, but it can easily be read as a standalone title and I hope you enjoy it as much as I did." ***Flippin' Pages Book Reviews***

"Ms. Campbell brings strong, caring, and intelligent women to the page that give me hope. She brings humor (the evisceration of Wicked Cousin Christopher is still making me giggle) and brightness to her characters. This is a lovely holiday story, perfect for an afternoon with snow falling and a toasty fire going." *5 stars, Buried under Romance*

"Anna Campbell has done it again, bringing two unlikely characters to life, and weaving their stories into romantic magic. Anthea's siblings were a delight, and the growing relationship between Anthea and her Lancelot just right. A wonderful, joyous read and such a pleasure stepping back in time to the 1800s." *5 stars. GoodReads Review*

"If you love Christmas historical romance books, put this one on your list." *5 stars. Amazon Review*

"Campbell always manages to create the perfect mix of sweetness and sass and scoundrels and romance with just the right amount of heat, and *Four Christmas Kisses* is an excellent example of that. You can see right away that these people should be a family and you can't wait to get to what you hope is an amazing happy-ever-after, but you're having too much fun and laughing too hard watching Christopher and Anthea flirt and fumble and pine and nearly test those Regency rule boundaries to want it to end too soon. I enjoyed this book so much. I recommend it as totally, completely satisfying any time of the year!" *5 stars. GoodReads Review*

ALSO BY ANNA CAMPBELL

Claiming the Courtesan

Untouched

Tempt the Devil

Captive of Sin

My Reckless Surrender

Midnight's Wild Passion

The Sons of Sin Series:

Seven Nights in a Rogue's Bed

Days of Rakes and Roses

A Rake's Midnight Kiss

What a Duke Dares

A Scoundrel by Moonlight

Three Proposals and a Scandal

The Dashing Widows Series:

The Seduction of Lord Stone

Tempting Mr. Townsend

Winning Lord West

Pursuing Lord Pascal

Charming Sir Charles

Catching Captain Nash

Lord Garson's Bride

The Lairds Most Likely Series:

The Laird's Willful Lass

The Laird's Christmas Kiss

The Highlander's Lost Lady

The Highlander's Defiant Captive

The Highlander's Christmas Quest

The Highlander's English Bride

The Highlander's Forbidden Mistress

The Highlander's Christmas Countess

The Highlander's Rescued Maiden

The Highlander's Christmas Lassie

A Scandal in Mayfair Series:

One Wicked Wish

Two Secret Sins

Three Times Tempted

Four Christmas Kisses

Scoundrels of Mayfair Series:

The Worst Lord in London

The Trouble with Earls

The Last Duke She'd Marry (2023)

The Duke Says I Do (2023)

Christmas Stories:

The Winter Wife

Her Christmas Earl

A Pirate for Christmas

Mistletoe and the Major

A Match Made in Mistletoe

The Christmas Stranger

His Christmas Cinderella (in the anthology A
Grosvenor Square Christmas)

Other Books:

These Haunted Hearts

Stranded with the Scottish Earl

Four Christmas Kisses

A Scandal in Mayfair Book 4

ANNA CAMPBELL

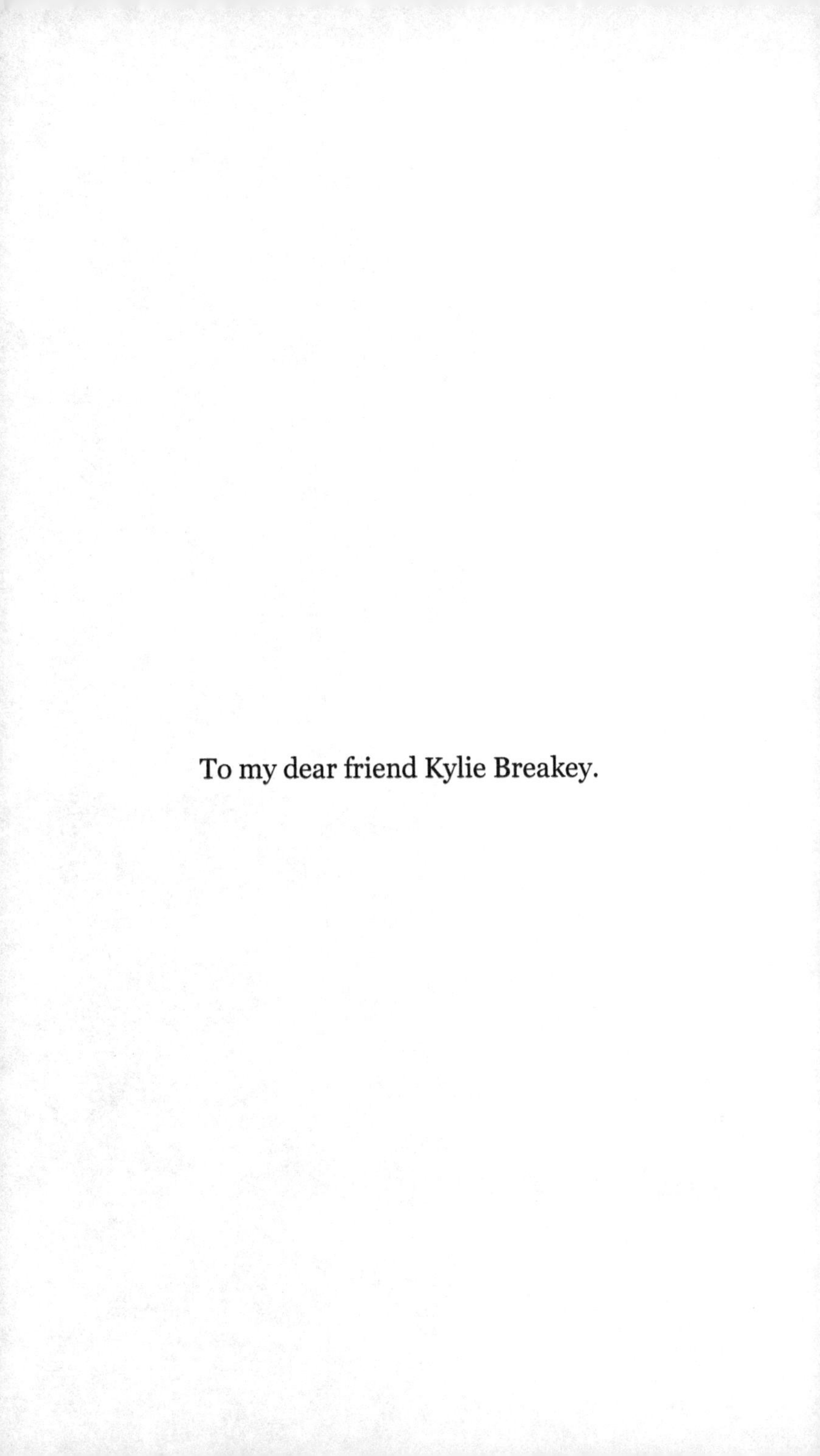

To my dear friend Kylie Breakey.

CHAPTER ONE

Yardley Woods, Shropshire, 19th December 1818

Snow, snow, snow. Everywhere Anthea Bryars looked, she saw snow.

The winter weather had delivered a frosty lead-up to Christmas. At this rate, she and her sisters wouldn't manage to get out of the house and down to the village church for the midnight service on Christmas Eve.

She wrapped her arms around herself and shivered, although she was muffled up in a wool scarf and a thick coat. The dreadful weather had kept her cooped inside all day with her sisters, and she'd been desperate for a breath of fresh air.

A short huff of amusement formed clouds in front of her face. Yes, fresh was an accurate description of this air. The walk had cleared her head, but half an hour outside in the freezing late afternoon made her think longingly of a pot of chocolate and a plate of hot scones back in Yardley Hall's cozy library.

She turned toward home. Around her, the trees were bare and silent, and the sky loured gray and heavy, promising more snow to come. A smooth carpet of white surrounded her as far as she could see.

Except...

She frowned and stopped mid-step. Something dark and large lay humped on the woodland floor, something that didn't look like a fallen branch or a rock.

What on earth? Shock held her motionless as her mind raced through the possibilities. Was it an animal? Or was it a log after all?

Curious and worried, she turned off the path. Using her staff, she made her way with difficulty toward the object. Although she soon realized that it wasn't an object at all. It was a person spreadeagled on the ground. A man wearing traveling clothes that marked him as an outsider and not one of the tenants.

Anthea struggled to hurry, but the thick snow made progress arduous. "Are you all right, sir?" she called out, still a good ten feet away.

If he was alive, she had to get him to shelter. Anyone ill or injured in these conditions wouldn't last long.

When he gave no response, fear colder than the air iced her veins. The nearest doctor was in Shrewsbury, ten miles away. It was too far to come in an emergency, even if the weather wasn't closing in.

What if the man was dead? For pity's sake, what was she to do with a dead stranger a few days before Christmas? And what in heaven's name was he doing here? The Yardley estate occupied an isolated valley well away from major roads or towns. Anyone who passed had business in the district. Nobody stumbled over her home by accident.

By the time she reached the man, she was panting and sticky in her heavy clothes, despite the frigid temperature. She fell to her knees beside the unmoving figure, grateful that the snow was firmer here. "Sir?"

Again, there was no answer. He lay flat on his face. A voluminous black greatcoat fanned out around him and good quality leather boots encased the feet sprawled across the white ground. He was bareheaded, and in possession of a disheveled mass of coal-black curls. His high-crowned hat lay upside down, a few feet from one outstretched gloved hand.

She turned her head and saw drag marks in the snow. More concerning, bloodstains splattered these signs of his progress.

"Sir? My name is Anthea Bryars. I live at the hall." She spoke loudly and slowly, hoping to rouse some response.

She took off her glove and curved her hand around the nape of his neck under his high collar. He felt dangerously chilled, but she didn't think he was dead. She prayed that wasn't just wishful thinking.

"Can I offer assistance?"

With increasing urgency, she battled to turn him onto his back. He was a big man, and once she saw his face, she realized he was handsome. And young. She'd guess no more than thirty. A sullen trickle of red marked his temple, although given the amount of blood that he'd shed reaching this particular tree, he'd been bleeding for a while.

"Sir? I need to get you back to the house, or you'll freeze to death."

She tapped his lean cheeks to return him to alertness, although she feared doing more damage. But she needed him to move. She couldn't carry him, and by the time she came back with help, he'd have succumbed to the cold.

At least she now knew that he was alive. His chest moved. And there was a trace of color in that haughty face, with its ferocious black eyebrows and slashing cheekbones and arrogant, aquiline nose.

"Please speak to me." She tapped a little harder, then gasped with surprise when amber eyes flickered open and regarded her with blazing fury from between thick black eyelashes.

"What in Hades are you doing, woman?" he snapped in the unmistakable tones of the upper classes.

Anthea sat back and returned his glare, as powerful relief rushed through her veins like the spring melt down the Severn. "Why, I'm trying to save your life, my good man. Under the circumstances, a spot of graciousness wouldn't go astray."

"Devil take you, you were punching me in the jaw."

Her lips tightened. "If you refuse to mind your manners, I'll leave you where you are."

It was an idle threat, and she suspected that this man knew it. The code of the countryside was to offer aid to stranded travelers. However rude they might be.

"Where's my horse?"

"I have no idea." She glanced around, but saw no hoofprints on the sea of white. "Can you stand?"

"Yes, I can bloody stand. I'm not an invalid."

"Very well." She rose and regarded him from above. Her experience of well-bred young men was limited, but she supposed that she couldn't blame him for being out of temper. He must be in pain and freezing, and perhaps she had been a little too enthusiastic in her efforts to wake him.

At least his grumpy reaction revealed that his head injury hadn't addled his wits. Those golden eyes were sharp and clear, and while his manners might need mending, his acerbic responses indicated that he wasn't seriously hurt.

He pushed himself up until he was sitting. She saw what that cost him. The color in his cheeks vanished, and his lips turned white. Her optimistic assessment of his condition suffered a blow.

"Will you lend me your stick?" His voice was strained.

Biting back the urge to tell him to say please, she passed it over and watched him struggle to his feet. His litany of muttered oaths made for interesting listening and broadened her education.

Without commenting, Anthea crossed to pick up his hat. She brushed off the snow and passed it to him. Despite the way his hand shook when he placed it on his head, he managed to set it at a jaunty angle. She waited for him to move. Instead he was weaving on his feet, and staring at her as if he'd never seen a woman before.

"Oh, for the love of heaven," she bit out and moved close enough to put her arm around his waist.

Straightaway, she was aware of contained male power, even now when he was on the brink of collapsing. She touched her sisters all the time, but this was different in every way. Her breath caught in her throat.

"I can..." he began in a shaky voice, his gloved hand closing around her stout staff in a deathly grip.

Anthea met glazed eyes in a milk-white face. A muscle jerked in his lean cheek, and his lips were thin with pain.

"No, you can't. Forget your blasted pride and rest on me."

"Not...gentlemanly."

She bit back a retort that acting the gentleman hadn't seemed his primary concern so far. "You can do the pretty, once you're capable of standing on your own two feet. I'll help you up to the house."

"Is it far?"

It was when she had to get an injured man there through the snow. "No. A few yards."

"Perhaps you should leave me behind and get your husband to assist me, then."

"No husband."

"Your father?"

"No father. No brother. Not even a brawny groom or gardener's boy. I'm the best that you're going to get, sir." She paused. "And I might have lied about the few yards, but I can't leave you out here. It's going to snow again, and we need to get you into the warm before you turn into an icicle."

The eyes that settled on her were once more alert, she was relieved to see. The effort of standing had tried his strength, but now that he was upright, he appeared to be managing. "Warm sounds good."

It did. When she'd been roaming about the woods, her mind stewing on her dilemmas, as it had stewed for the last month – and with the same lack of results – movement had kept her blood flowing. Now that she was standing in one place, cold seeped through the soles of her sturdy boots, and, despite her thick stockings, up into her bones. "Can you walk?"

"Yes." To prove it, he took an unsteady step and almost lost his balance.

He was a commandingly tall man, and he outweighed her by at least five stone, she guessed. When he staggered, he came near to bringing her down with him.

Anthea's worry sharpened, as she stood in front of him with her arms around him. If he passed out, she didn't have the strength to haul him to safety.

Panting, he leaned into her. More than leaned. He was close to falling. For a fleeting instant, her nose pressed into his chest. He smelled of snow and cold air, and as she breathed in, she caught other, more intriguing scents. Leather and horses and a hint of clean male.

"Careful," she gasped, her hold tightening.

"My apologies."

His manners seemed to be improving, too.

His arm slid around her waist, while his hand clutched her staff. It was almost an embrace and despite her difficulties, Anthea's heart performed a strange little flip.

"Let's try small steps. And the house is the other way."

For a fraught few seconds, he shifted to face the opposite direction. Anthea's attempts to maintain a suitable distance didn't outlast his change in position. By the time the stranger pointed the right way, she was cuddled up against him as if they were the best of friends. His arm circled her shoulders and hers curled around his waist. He was heavy, although she knew that he did his best to keep his weight on the stick.

"Apart from your head, do you have any other injuries?" she thought to ask.

That should have been her first question, curse her. After finding such a picturesque example of masculinity in her woodland, she'd been too taken aback to gather her thoughts. She prided herself on her good sense and unflappability. Lowering to discover that she was no better than a giggling girl when it came to an attractive man turning her upside down.

"My head is jangling. Otherwise I'm fine."

"You're bleeding."

"Am I?" He spoke as if it didn't matter.

"Yes, from your temple."

"I'll live."

Right now, she wasn't sure about that. Something about his careless tone told her that awareness receded. "You won't if you collapse again," she said with an edge that she hoped would focus his wandering attention.

"I won't collapse," he said with a scorn that she admired, however unconvincing it might be.

"Make sure you don't." She braced her arm against him. "Can you take another step?"

"Of course."

But there was no "of course" about it. He tottered toward the path that she'd followed on her walk. By the time they'd covered ten yards, they were both panting.

"This is hopeless," he grunted, slipping as he came to a precarious halt beside her. Luckily the snow here was dry and powdery, so he'd kept his balance. Mostly. A couple of times he'd clutched at Anthea's shoulder.

"Don't give up."

"If I fall, I'll take you with me." His arm slid free of her, and he straightened. The skin lay taut against the elegant bones of his face, and he was no longer white. He was gray. "I think I'll manage on my own, if I can build up a little momentum."

"Should I let you go?" she asked uncertainly.

He looked so determined. The chiseled jaw was set like stone, and something about his tense expression told her that he was in serious pain. "Yes."

"Head for that gate." She took her hands off him and gestured toward the wall that separated the garden from the woods.

Full of misgivings, she retreated and watched him proceed under his own power. He lurched forward and verged on falling. She heard another muttered curse.

But his resolution outweighed physical weakness. To her astonishment, he began to make progress, erratic but noticeable, toward the gap in the wall. He dug the stick deep into the snow and dragged himself forward more than he walked. For the first time since she'd found him, Anthea believed that she might get him back to the house.

CHAPTER TWO

The manor was in view before the man's halting, arduous trek came to an end. He planted the staff in the snow and slumped over it. His shoulders heaved as he struggled for breath, making clouds in front of his face. That gallant head bowed in a defeat that Anthea knew he'd resist admitting.

Odd how much she'd learned about him in their short acquaintance. An acquaintance not based on much conversation, at that.

He was brave and he was stubborn, almost to a fault. But there was something moving – if a little absurd – about his determination not to rely on her and to make his own way. He wasn't a whiner either, which gained her approval. As someone who had been forced to face life's vicissitudes, she'd learned how little use there was in complaining.

"It's not far now." She trudged up beside him and slid her arm around his waist. "If you put your arm around my shoulders, we should be inside in no time."

She waited for an objection, but his lonely, rather valiant travails had tried him to the limit. He trembled in her hold, but he made no attempt to pull away.

As an adult, she'd never been so close to a man. Her father had, by all reports, been an affectionate soul, and she had vague memories of him carrying her about and cuddling her. But he'd been gone for close to twenty years. Those recollections had nothing in common with what she felt when she supported this stranger.

At a slow shuffle, they set off through the kitchen garden, in this weather, a desolate expanse of lumpy snow. To her relief, the back door to the manor opened as she reached the steps. The man's raspy breathing and the obvious effort it took him to make even the smallest advance told Anthea that he came to the end of his strength. She was impressed that he'd coped as well as he had.

"Annie, I was getting worried." Her fifteen-year-old half-sister Harriet stopped and frowned. "Good heavens, who's that?"

"I have no idea." Anthea realized with surprise that while she'd found out so much about the man, she was yet to learn his name. "Help me get him inside. He's been hurt."

The man bit back a groan, as the stick clattered to the ground. Anthea had a suspicion that he'd lost track of where he was.

Harriet rushed down the steps and with her assistance, Anthea bundled the stranger into the kitchen. As they lowered him into a chair, he groaned aloud. He looked gaunt and ill, like a beautiful ghost. His eyes were closed, and he breathed in audible gasps. His head was bleeding again.

After Harriet rushed to shut the door, immediate and welcome heat enveloped

Anthea. She struggled out of her scarf, coat, and gloves and tossed them over another chair.

Anthea took off his hat, then his gloves. She chafed his large, elegant hands between hers, appalled at the iciness of his flesh.

"I suppose it makes a change from injured birds and stray cats," Harriet said, picking up Anthea's discarded clothing and arranging the items in front of the roaring fire to dry. "Where did you find him?"

"Out in the woods." Still rubbing his hands, she studied those aristocratic features for signs of recovery. "He'd collapsed under that big oak near the stream."

"But what the devil was he doing there? It's the middle of winter, and it's done nothing but snow. Anyway, nobody ever comes here. We're not on the way to anywhere."

Something Harriet spent a lot of time bemoaning. She was yet to learn the futility of protesting about what couldn't be changed.

Anthea had some sympathy with her sister's discontent. This wasn't much of a life for a vibrant young woman. And unless Anthea managed to come up with a solution to their current difficulties, the future that awaited Harriet was going to be even worse.

"I don't know why he was there. We didn't talk much. He mentioned a horse, so I'm guessing he was riding somewhere, got lost in the weather then fell off. When I found him, his mount was nowhere to be seen."

She felt a hint of warmth in his hands now, and the frightening gray pallor faded, she was pleased to see. Thank goodness, it seemed that they'd reached the house in time.

Harriet paused beside her and surveyed the man with unhidden curiosity. "He's very handsome."

"I hadn't noticed," Anthea said.

That prompted a dismissive snort. "Yes, you did."

Anthea hated the blush that flooded her cheeks. Because Harriet was right. She had noticed. "Well, perhaps I did, but his looks don't matter. He's a fellow creature in need."

Harriet sent her sister an unimpressed look. "You don't have to take the high moral ground all the time, you know. You're twenty-five, not eighty-five. You're allowed to notice a good-looking male when he falls at your feet."

Sometimes Anthea felt eighty-five, with the weight of the whole world on her shoulders. More so in the last month.

She didn't waste time arguing with Harriet's unflattering assessment of her character. Instead, she concentrated on practical matters. "Fill the kettle. We need to get him into a bed with a couple of hot water bottles as soon as we can. I don't know how long he was out there before I found him, but his skin is like ice."

Harriet didn't move straightaway. "He must be rich. His clothes are tailored within an inch, and those boots must have cost a pretty penny."

Harriet knew about fashion. She borrowed all the latest magazines from her best friend Polly Calthorpe, whose father was prosperous enough to subscribe to the papers. Anthea and her sisters scraped by on the rents from the estate, but harvests had been bad the last few years, and nobody had put any money into improvements since her stepfather's death.

"Harriet, hot water," Anthea said. "I need to clean that wound."

She dropped to her knees in front of the man. Those long legs sprawled across the flagstones on either side of her. As she pulled off his boots, she was vaguely aware of her sister bustling around the range.

His lack of response to her ministrations worried her. She couldn't help thinking that if she'd delayed her walk or taken a different route or avoided going out into the inhospitable weather at all, she would indeed have a corpse on her hands. She rose and started to unbutton the greatcoat.

"Who's this?" Eight-year-old Merry appeared at the entrance to the corridor leading back to the main part of the house. As usual, she had a book in one hand.

"We don't know," Harriet said. "Annie found him in the woods."

"I suppose it makes a change from a lost fledgling or a rabbit with a broken leg," Merry said, venturing closer. "He's very handsome. He looks like Sir Lancelot in my book."

Anthea resisted rolling her eyes. Just. "Merry, will you please go and make the bed in the blue room? We need to get him warm and comfortable as soon as we can."

"I'll come and help," Harriet said.

Anthea hardly noticed when her sisters left her alone with the stranger. He looked better than he had, but he remained deathly pale. His breathing was stertorous, and he hadn't stirred at all since he'd sunk into the chair.

Dear heaven, she hoped that he hadn't developed a chest complaint. As her sisters had half-humorously pointed out, this was a more challenging patient than the woodland creatures she was used to dealing with.

She rose and poured a bowl of hot water from the kettle, tempering its heat with a ladle of well water from a bucket. After picking up a clean cloth, she approached the man. She wanted a look at that graze on his head. While her medical expertise was based on the animal kingdom, and whatever ills and injuries her sisters and tenants incurred, she had some skills in healing.

With a gentle gesture, she brushed back a thick lock of black hair that fell across his high forehead. It was cold and damp and surprisingly silky to the touch.

Her hand stilled. Her sisters were right. He was an astonishing-looking man. She knew the illustration of Lancelot that Merry had referred to. The book was a family favorite, not least because of the dashing knights in the pictures. Most dashing of all was Lancelot with his saturnine beauty and faintly sulky expression. Even unconscious and injured, this man put Lancelot in the shade.

What on earth was such an Adonis doing, trespassing on their obscure patch of Shropshire? She could already tell that this was a man who belonged amongst the beaux of Mayfair. Or in some palatial house in the Home Counties. Not here at their shabby and isolated manor.

With careful efficiency, she began to sponge the blood from his temple. The scratch was long but shallow, she was pleased to see. At least it had stopped bleeding, although who knew what other harm his fall might have done? Harm that she couldn't see.

His eyes fluttered open again, the rich color of dark amber between those fans of thick black lashes. She wasn't sure that he was alert enough to notice that she mooned over him like a lovestruck fool, but heat stung her cheeks nonetheless.

"Sir, what is your name?" she asked, but he stared at her for a dazed instant before closing his eyes again. He'd exhausted his strength getting to the house. She prayed that his erratic alertness signaled nothing more serious than that.

Anthea spared a thought for his horse, lost in the snowy landscape. She hoped that it found shelter and food somewhere. Ordinarily she'd send the girls out looking for it while she cared for the patient, but night was falling and the snow had started up again just as she entered the house. Much as it went against the grain, she had to leave his horse to fend for itself.

Despite the heat, he hadn't stopped shivering. He needed to get out of those wet clothes and into a bed as soon as possible. She didn't want him suffering pneumonia as well as concussion.

"What's this I hear about you finding a stray gentleman in the grounds and bringing him home for our amusement?"

Anthea, who was doing her best to dry the man's mop of dark hair with a towel, while trying to avoid hurting him further, glanced up with relief as Winifred French bustled into the kitchen.

Originally her governess, Winifred had come to Yardley with Anthea's mother when she'd married Sir Lester Garland four years after her first husband's death. Since Anthea's mother had passed away five years ago, Winifred had stayed on to become the mainstay of the household.

These days, while she taught Anthea's sisters, she was more a member of the family than anything else. She was also, to Anthea's gratitude, a source of endless common sense.

"Winifred, thank goodness you're here. We need to get him upstairs, and I'm not sure I can manage on my own."

Winifred inspected the interloper. "By heavens, he's—"

"Handsome. Yes, I know."

Anthea hung the damp towel on a rack set up before the fire. "But I fear if we don't get him warm, he's going to be dead and handsome. I found him unconscious in the snow. Goodness knows how long he was out there."

"It can't have been too long, or he'd be dead already." Winifred took the kettle off the stove and emptied it into a tin jug that she covered with a lid to keep the heat in. "This is the worst winter I can remember since I came to Yardley."

As Winifred refilled the kettle and set it to boil, Anthea started to untie his neckcloth. It was sopping and bloodstained and cursed hard to untangle, but at last she managed it.

A strong throat emerged to her gaze as his damp shirt parted at the neck to reveal curls of dark hair on his chest. She was ashamed to feel something secret and feminine stir at the sight of his naked skin.

"Anthea, what's wrong? Is he still alive?"

She jerked in embarrassment, as she realized that she was staring rapt at that triangle of bare flesh. "Yes, I'm just wondering how we'll get him upstairs."

Winifred frowned at him, as if his height and splendid musculature were a personal affront. "There's a lot of him."

Anthea twisted her hands together as she studied the man. He hadn't stirred. Earlier acquaintance told her that he wasn't by nature so docile. "I wish I hadn't sent Jeb and Thomas home for Christmas."

The manor managed on a skeleton staff because Anthea and her sisters did most of the work to keep it functioning, but they had to employ two local men to do the heavy work.

"Too late to fret about that. Is he in a swoon?"

Those ferocious amber eyes opened to glare at Winifred with offended pride. Once, Anthea had tried to save a wild hawk with a broken wing. To her deep regret, she'd failed. Just so had the bird stared at her, with endless patrician contempt.

"Pray grant me some dignity, madam. I'm not fainting."

Winifred smiled. "No, I see that."

"Are you able to walk at all?" Anthea asked. "Miss French and I will do our best to help you up the stairs, but it would be useful if you could stand."

He curled long-fingered hands around the worn arms of the oak chair and pushed. To little effect.

Anthea stepped forward and extended her hands. "Here, hold onto me."

He regarded her with amused disdain. The way he switched in and out of awareness was troubling. A few years ago, one of the tenants' sons had fallen out of a tree and he'd displayed similar symptoms. Awake one minute. Insensible the next.

He'd died the next day.

As she took in this impressive being who had crashed into her life without warning, she promised herself that his injuries wouldn't defeat her.

"I must be twice your weight."

She set her jaw. "You can't stay in a kitchen chair all night."

"And I'm here to assist," Winifred said. "Courage, young man. I'm sure you're used to being lord of all you survey, but right now, you need to depend on a couple of women. We won't tell your society friends."

He regarded Winifred as if he didn't understand, and his hands loosened on the chair. Worried anew, Anthea seized his wrists. "Stand by, Winifred, just in case he falls."

"I won't fall," he said in a voice as rough as gravel.

"Ready?"

"Yes."

She tugged and thank goodness, he retained enough lucidity to help her, although once he was upright, she was alarmed at his unsteadiness. As he swayed, she put her arms around him. He was heavy, no surprise after the slog through the snow.

When he sagged, she braced to hold him up. He only just escaped collapsing onto the flagstone floor.

"Winifred, can you take off his coat? It's so wet, I'm sure it's making him heavier than he needs to be."

Removing his greatcoat proved difficult for Winifred and uncomfortable for the man, but he was lighter without the sodden weight of wool to hinder him. Under the heavy outer garment, he wore a stylish black fitted coat that wasn't nearly as wet.

"Take off this coat, too, Winifred," Anthea said.

Removing the black coat took further painful minutes. Wet wool was inclined to cling, even without taking the close fit into consideration. Harriet was right about the fine tailoring. His gray silk waistcoat was easier to get off, although Anthea feared that the expensive garment was ruined forever.

He bore the tugging and pawing with admirable stoicism, although by now she was familiar with the way his lips thinned when he was in pain. Once he was in his shirtsleeves, she and Winifred took their places on either side of him and helped him out of the kitchen, along the flagstoned corridor, and across the great hall to the wooden staircase.

"The room is ready," Harriet said from above them.

Anthea raised her head and smiled at her sister. "Thank you. Can you please stand aside until we get past, then go downstairs and bring up a bowl of warm water and some towels? We'll need to wash him."

A wash might restore some warmth to his flesh. She was conscious of how he shivered beneath the flimsy cambric of his shirt.

She'd chosen the blue room for their visitor because it was just off the landing. She and Winifred angled him through the door.

"Bless you, Merry," she said, as she saw the fire and the turned-down covers.

Her sister regarded the man with round eyes. "Is he going to die?"

"No, I am not," he said with commendable force.

"Will you please go down and help Harriet in the kitchen? There's a pot of soup in the pantry. Please heat that up. I baked today so there's fresh bread and a fruitcake and shortbread in the larder. You can both put a tray together."

Merry scuttled out of the room, as Winifred stepped back and regarded their guest with a critical eye. "We need to get him out of his clothes before he catches a chill."

"Damn it, I can manage." He did his best to stand unaided, although the hand that clung to the bedpost was white-knuckled with strain.

Winifred sent him a disapproving frown. "Language, young man."

To Anthea's surprise, that highbred face took on a sheepish expression. "Your pardon."

"We have some of Papa's nightshirts in the rag cupboard," Anthea said. "Do you want to go and get one?"

"You go and get it." Winifred sent her an equally disapproving look. "It's not suitable for you to undress our visitor."

"He's not in any state to—"

"Nonetheless, I'll take over from here."

Anthea put her hands on her hips and stood her ground. "I doubt you're any more experienced with disrobing young men than I am."

"That may be, my girl." Winifred pursed her lips, as she put her arm around the man's waist to keep him upright. "But I'm nearly forty years older than you are. The question of my virtue has long ago lost any importance. You however are still marriageable."

That made Anthea snort with amusement. "Not so you'd notice."

What did her reputation matter? Nobody was lining up to marry her. Even if they were, who was going to gossip about what the residents of the manor did in the middle of a snowstorm? The servants were all away for Christmas. The stranger himself floated in and out of consciousness. She was sure that even if she danced around him naked, he wouldn't blink.

"Anthea Bryars, I'll thank you to follow my instructions." It was the tone that always gained instant obedience from the younger Anthea. It retained its power. "Especially when our patient needs urgent care."

"Yes, Winifred," she said, afraid that despite her best attempts to hide it, her old governess had noted her improper interest in the stranger.

She was sorry to leave the room. She suspected that this was the most beautiful man who would ever cross her path. It would be interesting to see his body.

Purely for educational purposes, she told herself, without believing it.

An odd, restless warmth stirred in the pit of her stomach, at the thought of seeing him unclothed and placing her hands on his skin. Which was indefensible when he was weak and helpless and had no say in the matter.

To her relief, her stepfather's one remaining nightshirt was folded near the top of the rag pile. So near that Anthea suspected that it would have been washing floors within the week. She hurried back to the blue room in time to catch a peek of a lithe back and a pair of taut bare buttocks above long, powerful legs.

For a moment, the room receded and she felt as light-headed as the patient. He was like a statue come to life. A statue with a huge black bruise marring his ribs. She couldn't help wondering if perhaps he'd broken something when he fell off his horse. If he had, all this manhandling must be agony for him. No wonder he had difficulty clinging to consciousness.

Winifred looked up with displeasure, as she ran a damp flannel over his back. "Get out, Annie. This is no place for you."

He was rocking on his feet. Ignoring the reprimand, Anthea's fleeting distraction vanished. If he fell, she wasn't sure that they'd get him up again. She dashed forward and for a few manic seconds, all was activity.

Only when the man dropped groaning onto the bed did she have a chance to regret not seeing more of that spectacular body. By now, he was covered in her stepfather's billowing nightshirt which had been made for a man six inches shorter and twice as wide.

Despite her illicit curiosity, she was glad that he was dressed when Harriet and Merry trooped through the door with a tray of food and several hot water bottles. Her sisters were far too young to ogle a naked man.

"How is he?" Harriet asked, as Anthea took the hot ceramic flasks and began to line the bed with them, careful to keep them far enough away from the man so that he wasn't burned. He'd finally sunk into oblivion, and he didn't stir as she pulled up the quilt and adjusted the pillows.

The room was toasty warm, almost uncomfortably so. Yet as she'd struggled to get the nightshirt on him with Winifred's help, she'd noticed that his flesh remained clammy.

"He'll be better with rest and warmth and quiet," Winifred said, but the worry in her expression undercut any reassurance that answer might provide.

Merry set the tray on the chest of drawers against the wall. "Shall I give him his soup?"

"I think he's better off sleeping just now," Anthea said, although she wasn't sure whether he was asleep or insensible.

"Someone should sit with him," Winifred said. "Head wounds can be unpredictable. He might start fitting."

"I'll take first watch," Anthea said. "You all go downstairs and have dinner."

Outside it was dark. The short winter day had slipped away while they'd dealt with the crisis. The snow had closed in again, trapping them at the manor.

"I'll come back, once I've got the little ones settled into their beds." Winifred ushered the wide-eyed girls out of the room.

"Thank you," Anthea called after them.

Alone with the stranger, she couldn't help poring over those chiseled features, white as marble.

Who on earth was he? Men like him never came within her orbit. It would be a tragic outcome if this one entered her life, only to die in her care.

The determination that had saved countless birds and animals surged. He wasn't going to die. He was going to live, at least long enough to tell Anthea who he was and what brought him to Yardley Hall.

CHAPTER THREE

"*T*ake that! And that! And that, Wicked Cousin Christopher! This is our house. You can't come in. Stay out in the snow. I don't care if you're cold. You deserve it." What sounded like a violent clash of sticks followed.

Without moving – something told him that moving would be a very bad idea – Christopher Trant, Lord Denton, cracked open his eyes to see whether he was under attack.

To his surprise, a little girl perched on the end of his bed, holding a pair of carved wooden dolls. She smashed the toys together with a savage enthusiasm that, if her gleeful expression was any indication, provided enormous satisfaction.

One doll was dressed as a man and one wore a tattered skirt of indeterminate color. Christopher assumed that doll was female, although both were battered and hairless with rudimentary painted faces. At the moment, the female beat the male into defeat on the thick quilt covering Christopher.

"Die! Die! Die!" Three determined thumps on the luckless male doll before the child lifted the victorious manikin to her lips and kissed its worn face. "Ha! That's taken care of Cousin Christopher, Jenny."

He frowned. Was it coincidence that the defeated doll bore his name? He had a horrid inkling that it mightn't be.

"Poor Christopher," he said, his voice not much more than a croak.

"Great jumping Jericho!" The girl scrambled off the bed and regarded him with wide eyes. "You're alive."

His head ached like the very devil, which he supposed meant that he was alive. He tried to work out where he was. The room was large and light and rather shabby. Not somewhere that he'd ever been before, he could swear. Although events over the last little while were a blank, so he couldn't be altogether sure.

"I seem to be. Do I need to thank you for that happy state of affairs?"

The girl, about five or six he'd say, didn't answer. Instead, she stared at him as if he'd popped up out of nowhere. She was almost as shabby as the decor, although this was no pauper's dwelling and the child spoke with an educated accent.

He tried a simple question. "Where am I?"

"The blue room."

"And where is the blue room?"

"At our house."

Surely this child hadn't placed him in this bed. He had faint recollections of stumbling through the snow. "Are you alone here?"

"No, I'm with Christopher and Jenny."

The ache in his head intensified. "Christopher and Jenny?"

Her nod was solemn. "Yes. Jenny is very brave and Christopher is very bad. He wants to throw us onto the street, so that Harriet and Merry and I have to go to Great-Aunt Dorcas, and Annie will have to go out into the world to become a governess."

Christopher closed his eyes. The list of names made his head ring.

The child went on. "Actually Christopher used to be called Henry, but I wanted to play Kill Christopher so he had to change."

"I see."

He didn't. Not altogether.

The door opened to reveal a tall blonde woman who was vaguely familiar, although he wasn't sure why. Damn this fog in his brain. It made him feel as helpless as a newborn puppy.

"You're awake. Thank heaven." When a smile of heartfelt relief brightened her features, the site of Christopher's disturbance shifted from his head to his heart. By Jupiter, she was beautiful.

She glanced down at the child with a fond exasperation that looked marvelous on her. "Why on earth didn't you come and get me, Edwina?"

Edwina leveled a solemn gaze on the woman. "I had to kill Cousin Christopher first."

"That could have waited."

"But he was being specially evil."

The woman sighed. "I'm sure he deserved it, sweetheart."

The real Christopher hid a wince, as the girl nodded with all the mournful dignity of a hanging judge. "He did."

"But he's dead now?"

"He'll come back to life."

"That's good to hear. In the meantime, will you run downstairs and tell Winifred that our patient has opened his eyes and he must be hungry?"

"Yes, Anthea." The girl skipped out, taking the dolls with her. Christopher was glad about that.

There was something off-putting about watching his namesake receive such rough treatment.

"Actually I'm thirsty," he said, his voice still hoarse. Although now that he thought about it, he was hungry, too. "How long have I been here?"

"Two days." The woman – Anthea – walked forward and poured a glass of water from a jug on a chest of drawers. This must be the person destined to become a governess, according to what the little girl had said. That was a pity. Her air of calm authority made him think of a queen. That regal presence would be wasted when she became a downtrodden dogsbody in another woman's household.

She set the glass on the nightstand and bent over him. "Let me help you sit up."

Anthea proved even more delectable close up. Skin like rich cream. Deep blue eyes. Pink, generous lips. He wasn't sure that he was in any physical state to survive the sudden rush of his blood.

Christopher shifted in the bed in an automatic attempt to get closer to her and a groan escaped. "Blast it…"

Her pale brown brows contracted in concern. As he should have expected, the frown looked adorable on her. "Don't try and manage on your own. I understand that you like to be independent, but show some common sense. Hold onto me while I pile up the pillows."

That hinted that she knew him at least a little. The feeling strengthened that he occupied a mad world detached from his normal life.

Grabbing her arm, he was far too aware of his face pressed into her lush bosom. The scent of flowers and warm, nubile woman filled his nostrils. Despite his pain and weakness, his body stirred. He was definitely alive. A little too alive, given present circumstances.

For a few seconds that seemed to last both an eon and an instant of mingled pain and pleasure, he clung to her. She reached around him to heap up the pillows. All this jiggling made his head clang anew, but nonetheless, he was sorry when she carefully leaned him back.

"Let me go now," she murmured. "I'm sure that hurt, so take a second to get your breath back."

She sounded breathless herself. He supposed that she wasn't used to cuddling gentlemen to her bosom. He gathered that this was a household without men. If governessing was to be this winsome girl's fate, he could only assume that no fiancé or husband existed to offer her another option. That pleased Christopher, however much it puzzled him.

Even half-comatose, and after mere minutes in her company, he noted that this was a woman of exceptional attractions. Not an ingenue either. She must be only a couple of years younger than his own twenty-seven. Surely some local swain had seen what he had and offered to make this woman his wife.

Fighting to control his swimming senses, he slumped back and closed his eyes. He wanted to look at Anthea. He didn't want to retreat into the blackness that had held him captive for the last days. "Thank you," he said faintly, battling encroaching unconsciousness.

He supposed that he'd solve the mystery in time. That mystery, and all the others in this house. Right now, he felt too deuced weak and woozy to devote much thought to anything. Even a beautiful woman.

He must have passed out for a space, because when he opened his eyes, Anthea sat on the edge of the bed, holding a glass of water and inspecting him with more of that beguiling concern.

Christopher paused to take in more of her appearance. An oval face with large wide-spaced dark blue eyes, and a mouth that promised passion. Golden hair swept back in a severe knot, emphasizing the purity of her bone structure.

Like her sister – he assumed that Edwina was her sister, although there was little family resemblance – she was dressed in plain, good quality clothes that showed signs of frequent washing. In the faded green merino gown, she was lovely. Yet something in him itched to see her bedecked in rich silks and satins. Bright colours that brought out the subtle honey hue of her skin.

"Shall I help you drink?"

Even as ill as he felt, he wasn't going to knock back the chance for another cuddle. "Yes, please."

She shifted to put her arm around his shoulders and helped him to sit up straighter. "Shall I hold the glass?"

"No, I..." His hand knocked hers and a few drops of water spilled onto the covers. Damn it. He wasn't used to being feeble. He didn't like it, apart from the bit about snuggling up with this gorgeous creature.

The water felt like heaven on his parched throat. Nestling into Anthea's sweet-scented softness felt even better.

Before he was ready, she pulled the glass away.

"More please." His voice didn't sound quite so scratchy.

"See how that sits on your stomach first."

"I feel like I could drink the Thames dry."

Faint amusement made that full mouth twitch. "I'm sure."

"Where am I?" The drink also helped to clear his head. "I asked Edwina and she said the blue room, but I can see that."

Like the sisters' clothing, the furnishings were good quality, but old and well used. And the fabrics in this chamber were most definitely blue.

A laugh made Anthea move against him in a very pleasant way. "She's a confounded literal child. You're at Yardley Hall in Shropshire. The question I have is what you're doing here. We live in an isolated valley, and the weather has been awful. You must have had an important reason for traveling so close to Christmas."

Hell.

All of a sudden, so much made sense that until now hadn't. Although a thousand questions started to buzz around Christopher's addled brain.

It seemed that he'd reached his intended destination, despite his travails. Riding up from London, he'd made do with more and more inadequate inns as he ventured further from the capital. Two days ago, he'd decided to press on to Yardley Hall while the light lingered. It wasn't too far, and the heavy snow that had hindered most of his journey appeared to have let up.

He'd been eager to see the property that his uncle had left him. Not to mention that a trip to Shropshire saved him from visiting Morton House for Christmas, where his mother was becoming insistent that he find a bride and set up his nursery.

When they'd discussed the terms of the will, his uncle's lawyer had told him that he'd given the current tenants at Yardley notice to quit. Christopher had assumed the place must now be empty.

He berated himself for not checking further. He'd imagined the house had been let to some prosperous country gentleman, who would move onto another property where he'd make himself equally comfortable. It turned out that Christopher had been woefully wrong about that.

The "tenants" ended up being members of his family. That blasted useless solicitor hadn't been nearly careful enough with his terminology.

When he thought back to that violent confrontation between Edwina's dolls, he realized that he was indeed Wicked Cousin Christopher.

What a tangle.

He decided to play for time before he announced himself as the family villain. His accident gave him the perfect excuse. "I'm sure I did have a reason for being out, but I don't remember."

"Oh, no. I worried about your head wound." To his chagrin, Anthea released him and shifted until she could see his face. "Are you in pain?"

In fact, he felt better with every minute. Especially when Anthea embraced him. Although the water helped, too. "No."

She studied him with another faint frown wrinkling her brow. "You wouldn't tell me, even if you were."

Probably not. He hated feeling helpless at the best of times. Admitting his weakness to this enchanting girl made him grind his teeth. "I'd like some more water, if you please. I don't feel at all like I'm about to cast up my accounts."

"As you will." She rose to refill the glass before she returned to sit on the bed. He looked forward to her putting her arm around him again, but she merely extended the glass in his direction. "See if you can manage."

To his regret, he could.

She took the glass back. "Do you remember what happened two days ago?"

He did. A pheasant had flown out from a holly bush right under his horse's nose and Mistral had bolted. Tired after his long trip, Christopher hadn't been paying attention and despite his expertise as a horseman, he'd fallen flat on his arse. He'd tried to find his way back to the road, but he'd been hurt and dazed and he'd collapsed under a tree. When he stirred to alertness, a pretty girl was looming over him, insisting that he had to move.

That pretty girl regarded him now with a solicitude that he was a cad to enjoy when he was telling her a parcel of lies.

He strove to look vacant. "No, it's all a complete blank."

"That's not good news." She rose to her feet to return the glass to the chest of drawers. "I'll have to get Dr. Hobson back out to see you. When he visited yesterday, he said you were likely to wake in your own time and that once you did, you should have your wits about you."

Christopher hadn't had his wits about him since he'd stirred to find this rustic goddess observing him with her grave, beautiful eyes. "I'm causing you a lot of trouble."

She dismissed that with a wave of her hand. "In such an isolated place, it's our Christian duty to take in stranded travelers."

"You've done this before."

"Once or twice. Hardly anyone ever comes to Yardley. I hope you weren't out and about on a matter of life or death."

No, it had been an idle whim in an idle life. Something that he could already tell was outside Anthea's experience. "I'll try to remember."

"I think that tormenting yourself will delay your recovery. You've only just come back to us. Perhaps you'll remember soon. Do you know your name?"

Yes, he did. To his even stronger regret, his name was Wicked Cousin Christopher. Did that mean that he and this girl were kin?

He scrunched up his face, as if battling to bring his identity to mind. "No, I'm sorry."

Christopher should feel like a swine for the dreadful lies that he told, but when she stepped forward to place one white hand on his forehead, all he could do was bask in her touch.

"You don't have a fever. I was worried that you might take a chill after lying in the snow."

He had good reason to thank the rugged Trant constitution. He'd feared that he might be ready to stick his spoon in the wall, when he'd been staggering around the icy wilderness, bleeding and confused.

"You saved my life." For once, he was in earnest. "How can I ever thank you?"

She looked flustered, which charmed him, because he'd already noticed that she was a supremely capable woman. "Not at all."

"Yes, you did. Can you tell me your name?"

"Anthea. Anthea Bryars."

Bryars? He sifted his memory for some family connection, but nothing came to mind. Perhaps his assumptions were mistaken, and Miss Bryars was a servant of some sort. Yet she didn't act like a servant, and she'd been comfortable ordering Edwina about. "Is that delightful little girl your sister?"

That delightful little girl who he knew wanted to spiflicate him. He hid a wince, as he recalled her bloodthirsty relish when she pounded Wicked Cousin Christopher into submission.

A dismissive huff of laughter escaped Anthea. "You really did take a knock on the head. Edwina is a handful. She always has been. I doubt anyone would call her delightful."

"A young lady of very decided opinions."

Anthea rolled her eyes. "Yes, that's true. And, yes, she is my sister. Or at least my half-sister. Mamma married Sir Lester Garland after my father passed away when I was a little girl."

Ah, Christopher started to make sense of the connections. To his relief, this alluring woman was no blood relation at all.

Sir Lester Garland had been his uncle. Christopher had never met the fellow, although he'd known and liked Basil Garland, Lester's younger brother, the man who had bequeathed Yardley Hall to him. Basil had been a disreputable middle-aged roué with an unexpectedly kind heart. Allowing his brother's orphan child to remain in the house wasn't out of character. He'd also been remarkably absent-minded, so failing to make some provision after his death for Anthea and Edwina wasn't out of character either.

In fact, Christopher hadn't had the slightest idea that Sir Lester had had children. He'd assumed that the man had died without issue, because his brother inherited the baronetcy and the estate. If Sir Lester only left a daughter behind, that explained the disposal of the estate. Basil had never married. He'd had a weakness for the gentle sex, but he hadn't been a one-woman man.

A knock at the door, and Anthea rose from the bed to admit an older woman carrying a laden tray. Good God, could this be Sir Lester's widow? The situation became more complicated by the minute. Anthea hadn't said anything about her mother passing away.

Anthea smiled at the woman with open affection. "Winifred, I'm sure our patient is glad to see you."

Christopher's mouth watered, as he caught a waft of savory scents from the food on the tray. He felt like he hadn't eaten in a week, even if he couldn't help ruing the interruption to his time alone with Anthea.

"He's well enough to eat?" the woman asked.

"My oath, I am," he said.

"That's a good sign." Winifred set the tray on the chest. "And who am I addressing?"

"He doesn't remember his name," Anthea said, her smile fading. "Or why he was in the valley. He must have got lost in that terrible snowstorm."

"Hmm," Winifred said, and Christopher wasn't quite sure what the noncommittal sound meant.

Anthea turned to him. "This is Miss Winifred French, my old governess who lives with us here."

Christopher had already worked out that this couldn't be Anthea's mother – partly because this woman was too old to be Edwina's mother, too. Winifred must be at least sixty. "Good afternoon, Miss French. I apologize for putting you to all this inconvenience."

"Hmm," the woman said again. "Would you like some soup?"

"I'd rather have a steak."

Anthea frowned at him in censure. Even disapproval looked superb on her. "I'm sure you would, but Dr. Hobson said that when you wake up, we should serve you something light. Sometimes concussion causes nausea."

He remembered feeling sick as he'd struggled through the snow at Anthea's side. But right now, all he felt was hungry. And in need of a shave. The bristles on his cheeks were deuced itchy.

"Shall I feed you or do you think you can manage?" Anthea's sympathy warmed his heart. As a rule, he loathed being ill, but he most definitely didn't loathe being the center of her attention.

"I'd hate to spill soup everywhere."

Miss French cast her a sharp glance. "It's more appropriate for me to take over now. As I said to you when I undressed him, you shouldn't be alone with this young man, my girl. He's not a pigeon with a broken wing or an orphaned fox cub."

Anthea blushed. Christopher must continue to suffer the effects of the bang on the head. The poetical thought struck him that the rosy color flushed her skin like sunrise brightened the dawn sky. When he'd never suffered a poetical thought about a woman in his life.

"He's not well," Anthea said. "When someone's in trouble, their needs outweigh silly rules about propriety. Who's to know or care what I do?"

He'd already noticed the threadbare nightshirt he wore. The idea of Anthea removing his clothes was exciting. The idea of Winifred undertaking the duty wasn't half as titillating. While he remembered nearly everything since he'd ridden onto the Yardley estate, he couldn't bring to mind what had happened once he reached the house.

"I know and I care," Miss French said in an uncompromising voice.

"I'm very respectable," he said, trying to sound as harmless as a toothless old dog.

It wasn't altogether true. Not to mention his reputation in this house as Wicked Cousin Christopher. But he knew his duty as a gentleman, and despite Anthea's refreshingly forthright manner and outmoded clothing, it was apparent that she was a virtuous woman of standing. Even if he was in a fit state to seduce her, he'd have to think twice about it.

Or at least he would, if she didn't encourage him. Dear God, let her encourage him.

Winifred glowered at him. "But how can you be sure, if you don't know who you are? You could be a notorious brigand for all we know. Or a thief. Or a murderer."

"I'm sure he's not," Anthea protested.

"I'm sure I'm not, too," he said, trying even harder to sound and look innocent of nefarious intentions. The problem was that while he wasn't guilty of Winifred's accusations, when it came to Anthea, his conscience wasn't lilywhite.

"Well, even if you are, you'll have to deal with me and I'm quite formidable – and disinclined to melt into a puddle, just because a pretty young fellow cares to give me the eye."

"Winifred!" Anthea was blushing like fire now. "That's enough."

Christopher studied her with interest. He rather liked the idea of this intriguing beauty melting into a puddle when he smiled at her.

He caught Winifred's eye and smiled. "Does that mean you think I'm handsome, Miss French?"

His attempt to charm her fell flat. She shot him a stern look. "Handsome is as handsome does, young sir. Now let me give you your soup before it gets cold. I'll see you downstairs, Anthea."

"Yes, Winifred," she said in a suitably docile tone and to Christopher's regret, she left the room.

CHAPTER FOUR

*D*espite Christopher's brave words about devouring a steak, he only managed half a bowl of beef broth and a slice of bread and butter before he dropped off to sleep.

Winifred wasn't much of a conversationalist, so he didn't find out much from her. Apart from the fact that she was immune to all efforts to win her over.

The beauteous Anthea Bryars didn't reappear, much to his frustration.

He must have slept after that, deeply and without dreaming. When he stirred, it was to the sound of a hushed conversation in the far corner of the room.

His eyes flickered open to reveal candlelight. Anthea was out of his view, talking to a man over near the window. Christopher had drifted off under Winifred's gimlet stare, but the formidable older lady wasn't in evidence.

He was about to let Anthea know that he was awake when he caught the gist of the conversation.

"If you marry me, Anthea, all your problems will be over. You can stay nearby, the girls will have a home, and you'll have a suitable place in the world."

Christopher was astonished at the rage that gripped him. How dare this encroaching upstart, whoever the hell he was, propose to Miss Bryars? Trying not to move, he strained his ears to hear her response.

She sighed. "Dr. Hobson—"

"Philip."

She sighed again. "Philip, I don't love you."

Relief flooded Christopher. That should put the sod in his place.

Christopher's relief was short-lived. "You can learn to love me. On my part, there's no lady in the world who I esteem as much as I esteem you."

"Thank you. You're a valued friend, and I respect and admire you—"

"That's the start of love."

"I'm not sure."

"You aren't experienced with such things, my dear. You should accept my guidance on this matter."

Anthea gave a huff of laughter. "Philip, you've been our family doctor for ten years. When have you ever known me to take guidance from anyone? I fear I'd be a troublesome wife, who insists on having her own way."

Take that. Christopher wanted to cheer her.

"You're a woman of will and intelligence. If you think I don't appreciate that, you underestimate me."

"I don't underestimate you, Philip. It's because I value you so highly that I hesitate to enter into a marriage, when I can't promise to love you as you deserve."

"If I'm satisfied with the bargain, that should be enough."

"And our situations are so unequal. I'd always owe you my gratitude for taking me as your wife, when I bring neither fortune nor connections to the match."

"I don't care about that. Anyway, if we're talking about birth, you're a baronet's daughter, whereas my father was a humble apothecary. Many people would say you were condescending to marry me."

"Being a baronet's daughter doesn't put food on the table or a roof overhead. For me or for my sisters."

"If you marry me, you'll have your own home and a husband who loves you and a respected place in Shrewsbury society. My situation is prosperous and promises to become more so, when I take over Dr. Willoughby's practice in the New Year. You would want for nothing. You'd have a secure future. You and your sisters."

"But that's yet another obligation you're accepting."

"They're good girls."

"When they're asleep. Maybe. There's Winifred, too. You'd accept responsibility for a houseful of people to whom you owe nothing. It seems jolly unfair."

"If I wed you, the reward makes up for everything else."

"It would be wrong, Philip."

"How so, given I know what I'm signing up to?"

"But I don't think you do. In wedding me, you're taking on four other people. It's too much to ask."

The man was starting to sound a bit harried at the way she countered all his persuasion. "So you'd rather seek a position as a governess and waste all your beauty and spirit in the service of another woman's children, when you could have your own family and home? You're happy to see the girls sent away to an unloving aunt and a school that will keep them apart? And what about Winifred? She's too old to have to seek new employment."

"You know that's not what I want," Anthea said in a low voice weighted with such anguish that Christopher couldn't help but feel a pang of guilt. Not the first, but by far the most painful. His thoughtlessness had placed this admirable lady in this bind.

"I know it better than you think. So put aside your pride, Anthea, and say you'll marry me. No woman will be more cherished."

"But I still don't love you, Philip," she said in despair, and Christopher's gut clenched with denial as he heard that she was weakening.

"You'll come to love me."

"You're worthy of love, but I don't think it arrives just for the wishing." Her voice lowered even further, so Christopher almost didn't hear her. "My parents loved each other. I'd always hoped that I'd find a similar bond with the man I married."

"So for the sake of a misplaced romantic notion, you're happy to say goodbye to the girls and submit to a life of servitude?"

"How could I be happy about it?"

"Then marry me, Anthea. Marry me, and all your difficulties will be over."

"All my difficulties, except my conscience kicking up a storm because I took shameless advantage of you and your generosity."

Good God, she was on the verge of accepting. The clodhopper doctor must hear that, too. "If I enter the arrangement with my eyes open, what's the crime?"

"Philip, I..."

"Say yes, Anthea."

Christopher was just about to make a noise to disrupt the conversation when she answered. Not with a final refusal, damn it, but enough to offer the doctor a reprieve. "It's only a few days until Christmas. Our last Christmas here at Yardley. Perhaps the last Christmas when we'll all be altogether, my sisters and Winifred and I. Let me think about your proposal and give you an answer on Boxing Day."

"Anthea, you'll never be sorry you took me." The fellow clearly thought that she would agree. Christopher couldn't argue with that conclusion, much as he might wish to.

"I'm not promising anything. I ask you to leave me to consult my own judgement in peace until then."

"Very well." He sounded reluctant. He, like Christopher, must hear how she wavered. The doctor must guess that if he persisted, he might get the answer he wanted.

It sounded as if her situation was desperate. Christopher gave her credit for her principles, if not her common sense, in holding back from seizing the lifeline that Dr. Hobson offered. He supposed that he also should commend the sod for not pushing for an acceptance when he was so close to getting one.

The doctor went on. "I'll propose again on Boxing Day, when I hope you'll make me the happiest of men."

"I'll give you your answer then," Anthea said.

Christopher recognized her tone as resignation. By God, she'd end up taking the bugger. Everything within him rose up in outrage.

He could always tell her who he was and say he was willing to let her and her sisters stay at Yardley. That would save her from marrying the doctor.

Yet some instinct told him to find out more before he admitted the truth. So far, she'd treated him with appealing informality. If he admitted that he was in fact Wicked Cousin Christopher, would she retreat from the possibility of friendship – and more than friendship? Even worse, would she decide that she hated him as Edwina did?

He'd like a clearer idea of the situation before he confessed his identity. In fact, he'd like to take a look at the manor and get some idea of his inheritance, before he made any decision about its future. After all, that was why he'd ridden all this way through the winter weather.

What harm would it do if he pretended to a faulty memory for another day or so?

"What do you think about the man's lack of memory, Philip?" Anthea asked, sounding thankful to change the subject. "He seems unharmed otherwise, apart from the bruises you saw when you visited yesterday."

"Concussion can cause patchy recollection. What you told me about helping him back to the house and the way he drifted in and out of consciousness hints that he took a hard knock. Usually though, it's only the events just prior to the impact that remain unclear. You say he's unable to recall his name?"

"Or any other details of his identity. I can't help feeling that someone somewhere is worried sick about him."

It struck Christopher as a pity that she was so wrong. A few days before Christmas, someone should be waiting for him and missing him. But nobody was. Even his mother was too preoccupied with her own concerns to regret his absence.

"His horse hasn't turned up?"

"No. We all went out looking yesterday when there was a break in the snow, but as you know, the blizzard came in again after a couple of hours. I hope the poor beast found shelter with one of the tenants, but in this awful weather, nobody will want to come to the house to report a lost horse."

"If we find his mount, we might also find luggage and some identification."

"You don't think his memory will come back by itself?"

Christopher suffered another twinge of guilt as he heard the worry in her voice.

"I hope it will. I'm far from easy about his condition. Perhaps I should take him back to my house for observation."

Like hell.

To his relief, Anthea didn't agree. "I can't see that jolting him all the way to Shrewsbury in the snow will do him an ounce of good. He's better where he is. He's only been awake a day. It's too early to panic."

"But what if he starts fitting? Or he falls into a swoon? Should I stay?"

Christopher didn't like that idea either. He wanted Anthea nursing him, not her lowborn suitor.

"That's very kind, but you have family coming for Christmas."

"You think I'll be a burden, when you already have your hands full with the girls. You were too generous, letting all the servants go home for Christmas."

"Philip, you're not my husband yet," she said firmly.

Christopher wanted to applaud. Not least because she refused to put the doctor up for the night.

"I'm sorry. You're right. But I hate to think of you slaving away."

She gave a faint laugh. "Slaving is a little strong. And I have help."

"From three useless chits and an ageing governess. You deserve better."

"My sisters aren't useless, and I rely on Winifred's wisdom and help. You're unjust."

"How can I sleep at night, when you have a strange man in the house? You know nothing about him. He could be a murderer or a criminal."

"He could," Anthea said in a doubtful tone. "But so far he's shown no signs of being anything but a gentleman who got lost in the snow."

"So far, he's been suffering the effects of concussion. What happens when he's back on his feet? It isn't proper for a lone man to have free range of a household full of women."

"There are plenty of chaperones."

"I still don't like it."

"Philip..."

Christopher wasn't alone in hearing the warning in her tone. The doctor sighed. "My word, you're a stubborn woman, Anthea Bryars."

"I am. Which makes it a puzzle why you want to marry me."

His laugh was rueful. "You have plenty of other qualities that make you irresistible."

For his part, Christopher admired her strength. It sounded like she'd had to handle numerous difficulties and responsibilities. She'd needed courage and determination to survive.

It was time he brought this conversation to an end. He gave a realistic groan and rolled onto his back in the bed.

"He's waking up." Again Christopher heard relief in Anthea's voice. "Perhaps his memory has returned."

Not now, when Christopher had identified a rival, it hadn't. He didn't know what he wanted of Anthea Bryars – apart from the obvious, that was – but he didn't like the idea of her marrying some obscure country doctor.

"How are you feeling?" Anthea came across to rest her cool white hand on his forehead. "You still don't have a fever, thank goodness. I was afraid you'd get pneumonia."

He loved her touch on his skin. He wished that he could prolong it. But to his regret, she lifted her hand away.

"My headache is better, thank you." Since he'd come back to consciousness yesterday, he'd been in pain, but today that receded to a dull throb. He didn't have to try to add a husky edge to his voice. Her touch had made his throat close with longing.

She brought him a glass of water. "That's good."

With difficulty, he pushed himself up against the pillows. He took the glass and managed to sip with commendable deftness. His hand was steadier now, thank heaven. He'd hated fumbling around like a clumsy oaf. Most of all in front of a pretty girl who he'd much rather impress.

"Do you remember anything?" she asked.

"I remember everything since I woke up in this room yesterday."

She frowned in concern. "So you still don't know your name or where you came from?"

"No, I'm sorry."

She sighed. "You must be so distressed to be confused and alone with strangers. Especially so close to Christmas. I wish I could help."

He bit back a protest at being called a stranger, although of course he was. Even if he didn't want to be.

"Thank you." He added a silent apology for deceiving her. Which didn't make him any more inclined to reveal his identity.

"Dr. Hobson is here to see you. He came the day after I found you, although I suspect you don't remember."

"I don't." At least he could tell the truth about that.

Anthea took the empty glass and stepped aside to allow the doctor to approach the bed.

Christopher knew it was unworthy – a lot of what he did right now was unworthy – but he wanted the doctor to be five feet tall, preferably with a walleye and a paunch. But the man who approached him was almost as tall as he was, and he looked like bloody Young Lochinvar, with gilt hair and bright blue eyes. The sight of this local Apollo made Christopher feel sicker than he'd felt since he'd woken up yesterday.

"Anthea, I should examine my patient in private." Dr. Hobson surveyed Christopher with an antipathy to match his own.

"As you wish. I'm sure he's hungry. I'll go and see what we've got in the kitchen."

"A steak?" Christopher asked hopefully.

Hobson regarded him without pleasure. "No, better that he stays on light, bland food while his wits are scrambled."

Christopher would dearly love to scramble this jackanapes's wits. "That's no food for a red-blooded man."

"Nonetheless, it's safer. Head wounds need careful nursing."

"More broth then," Anthea said and laughed when Christopher grimaced.

She had a lovely laugh, and he liked the teasing light in her eyes. Hobson however was less in favor of these signs of amity between Anthea and her charge. He shot her a narrow-eyed glare. "The patient needs rest and quiet."

"Yes, Philip," she said, instantly sobering.

"No excitement. I believe Miss French is the perfect nurse."

"Winifred has already done a lot of the work, but she's not as young as she was. I don't want her sitting up all night."

"Anthea—"

"Philip, I'm not going to argue with you. Harriet is old enough to help, and she's already doing her part."

"Very well." He must hear the same finality in her tone that Christopher did, because he accepted her decision. With reluctance.

Anthea sent Christopher an encouraging smile that had his heart flipping over like a damn circus mountebank. Heaven help him, she was delicious. It was a crime to leave a woman like her to rot away in this backwater. "I'll bring up a tray in a few minutes."

He smiled back with delight. "Thank you."

Too much delight. Anthea missed Hobson's suspicious glance, but Christopher didn't.

"Can you walk?" Hobson asked flatly, once they were alone.

"I can make it to the chamber pot and back." He'd needed help the first few times, but he was stronger today than yesterday. To his great annoyance, he remained as weak as a kitten, although at least his head felt sharper.

To his relief, when he'd first got onto his feet to empty his bladder, Winifred had been on duty. Every cell of his body protested at the idea of the ravishing Anthea performing such a private service for him.

"Any light-headedness when you stand?"

"Some." More than some, but he hated admitting his weakness to this presumptuous nobody.

"And no glimmer of memory?"

Was that a trace of disbelief in the doctor's voice? "None."

"I'm sure it will come back. I hope when it does, you remember that you're a gentleman who understands the respect and gratitude that he owes to Miss Bryars and her family for taking you in."

Hobson might as well say, "Keep your hands off Anthea."

"I'm well aware of my obligation to Miss Bryars for her kindness and care," he said with a hint of aristocratic hauteur.

The lordly tone didn't have much effect on Hobson. "Make sure you don't forget that then, along with everything else."

The man began to poke and prod at Christopher. While Hobson might want to make things as uncomfortable as possible, Christopher gave him reluctant credit for his gentleness. However much he wanted to despise the blockhead, it was more difficult than he wished.

"I'd like to send you on your way, but until we know who you are and where you were going, that's not safe. I wouldn't be doing my medical duty if I made you leave now."

For a moment there, Christopher had almost been in charity with the quack. The pompous tone and barely hidden hostility put paid to that, quick smart. The fellow acted as if he owned Yardley Hall, when in fact he was trespassing on Christopher's property. A convenient recovery of his memory would put this nonentity in his place.

However, announcing his identity would destroy the warmth developing between him and the family, especially Anthea. So he restricted himself to an ironic agreement. "Good for you."

Hobson's eyes narrowed. "Don't imagine this household is full of unprotected and helpless females."

"I wouldn't call Miss Bryars helpless. She seems a most capable lady."

"She is. But she also has a soft heart. I'd hate anyone to take advantage of her."

Anyone, meaning Christopher. "I have no intention of trespassing on Miss Bryars's good nature."

"See that you don't." The assurance hadn't convinced Hobson. To be fair, Christopher wasn't sure that it convinced him either. "Miss Bryars isn't alone in the world. She and I are to be married."

Christopher had heard enough to know that wasn't true. Or at least it wasn't set in stone.

Poor Anthea was in a difficult position, and he couldn't blame her for considering the swine's proposal. He sent the doctor a straight look, even as he silently consigned him to Hades. "I struggle to take ten steps on my own two feet. Even if I had depraved intentions, which I don't..." *Liar, liar, liar.* "...Miss Bryars could fight me off with one hand. For pity's sake, Edwina could knock me down."

"But you're stronger every day." Hobson's taut expression didn't relax. "I'm just advising you not to interpret Miss Bryars's natural concern for her fellowman as anything more than her Christian duty."

"Miss Bryars likes me, and she's a clever woman."

"She is. But her experience with wealthy gentlemen is limited. I would ask you to have a care." He paused. "We don't know who you are. Dear God, *you* have no idea who you are. You could be committed elsewhere. You could be married. You don't belong here, and the sooner you're on your way, the happier I'll feel."

Good Lord, the poltroon was warning him off in no uncertain terms. Had he seen some sign that Anthea harbored an inappropriate interest in her patient?

Now there was a devilish encouraging thought. Christopher had feared that he'd made such a poor show that she might pity him, but never admire him. Had he got that wrong?

Anthea appeared with his lunch and saved him from replying. "How is our patient?"

Hobson cast Christopher a sour glance. "He'll live." He spoke as if that was no cause for celebration.

"I'm so glad." She laid the tray on Christopher's lap and gave him another of those heart-stopping smiles. "If he doesn't, we'll have to keep his body in the cellar. The ground is too frozen to bury him."

That made Christopher laugh. "No need to sound so jolly about the prospect."

CHAPTER FIVE

*C*hristopher fell into another deep sleep after his meal. The life of an invalid grated. He was used to being strong and active.

When he stirred, he found himself under the observation of two pairs of solemn blue eyes. Two pairs of unfamiliar blue eyes, although he could guess who they belonged to. Anthea had mentioned that she had three sisters to care for, when she'd fended off a proposal from that overweening sawbones. That indicated that Christopher had two more cousins at Yardley, beyond Edwina with her homicidal impulses.

"Did we wake you up?" the younger girl, who he guessed was about eight or nine, asked. The two girls sat on wooden chairs beside the bed and studied him with unwavering interest.

"No."

"We tried to be very quiet." The other girl was older, about fifteen. He remembered her from his hazy recollections of the night when he'd arrived. Neither of the girls looked like Anthea, although they bore a resemblance to dark-haired Edwina.

Feeling at a disadvantage, he raised himself against the pillows. "Thank you."

"Do you remember your name yet?" the younger girl asked.

"No, I don't. Will you tell me who you are?"

The older girl answered. She showed the promise of beauty, although in a very different style from Anthea. "I'm Harriet Garland, and this is my sister Meredith."

"But everyone calls me Merry," the girl said. "Which is odd, because I'm not. Very merry, I mean. I've always got my nose in a book."

He'd already noticed the thick volume of tales of King Arthur on the floor beside her chair. "I read that one."

Merry's smile was charming and reminded him of Anthea. "It's good, isn't it?"

"It inspired a thousand sword fights."

Harriet regarded him, transfixed. "You do remember something."

Hell, he needed to be careful. "I think it's the same way that I remember how to use a knife and fork, or to say please and thank you."

Merry seemed to accept that, but Harriet studied him like a bug under a magnifying glass. "Those are general things. What you said was more specific."

It was. He and his brother had spent hours pretending to be knights of the Round Table. His brother, who was tucked up at his mother's house, preparing for a family Christmas. David was younger and hadn't inherited the title, so nobody was pressuring him to marry.

Christopher gave a theatrical wince and closed his eyes. Luckily, Merry took the hint. "Annie said we weren't to pester him, Harry."

"Would you like some water?" Harriet asked. "We're meant to be nursing you."

He opened his eyes. "Yes, please," he said in a failing voice, hoping to discourage further questions.

Merry leaped to her feet and poured him a glass of water. "Do you need me to hold it for you?"

"No, I can manage. Thank you." He yawned. Which was mad, considering how much he'd slept since his accident.

Despite his self-serving pretense at being in pain, he was feeling better. All this sleep seemed to help, despite it leaving him thickheaded. So thickheaded that he'd almost given himself away.

He took the glass and swallowed a mouthful, as Merry returned to her chair. Both girls continued to stare at him as if he was about to transform into a fire-breathing dragon.

"I'd be terrified if I lost my memory," Harriet said.

"Dr. Hobson says it will come back."

"Dr. Hobson is very clever," Merry said.

"And very handsome," Harriet added.

Christopher bit back a growl, although it was true. Plague take the man's classic features.

"He wants to marry Anthea," Merry volunteered.

"Does she want to marry him?" Christopher asked, pretending to a casual interest.

"If she marries him, we can all stay together," Merry said. "We have to leave this house after Christmas."

"Actually our wicked cousin wanted us out at the beginning of December." Harriet's voice hardened. "Who throws a family out into the snow just before Christmas?"

More of the wicked cousin business. Christopher's conscience cringed. The solicitor should have told him about the girls. And Christopher should have asked a few more questions, damn it.

"But Anthea said we'd stay for one last Christmas in our home," Merry said. "She said if Wicked Cousin Christopher turned up to evict us, she'd fight him off with Papa's old pistol."

Startled, Christopher stared at the girl. "She'd shoot...the fellow?"

These two girls – his cousins, he supposed – were too disarming. He'd come close to saying "me" instead of "the fellow."

Harriet leveled a scornful, older-sibling frown on her sister. "She was joking."

Merry's jaw set in a stubborn line. "I don't think so. She was so angry when she got the letter from Uncle Basil's lawyer, telling us we had to get out in two weeks. Nothing more. No expression of sympathy for the loss of our uncle. No questions about where on earth we were going to go. As she said, we're family. The least Cousin Christopher could do is try to make some arrangements for us. Or come to Shropshire and tell us himself that he doesn't give a fig what happens to his blood kin."

Since his arrival, Christopher's conscience had often smarted. But this discussion delivered a mortal wound to his self-satisfaction. Awkward and uncomfortable to discover at the age of twenty-seven that he was a selfish swine.

Merry was right – and surprisingly articulate for a girl of her age. Anthea was right, too. He deserved shooting.

"Cousin Christopher doesn't know us," Harriet said.

"That doesn't matter," Merry retorted. "Blood is thicker than water."

It was. Christopher might curse the lawyer's incompetence, but he knew the real blame for this mess lay at his door. He should have spent a little more time and care finding out about his legacy.

"So where are you all going to go?" Edwina had given him some idea, but these girls were old enough to know the details.

"If Anthea marries Dr. Hobson, we'll move into Shrewsbury to live with them," Merry said glumly.

Over my dead body.

"You don't sound very enthusiastic." Christopher tried not to find that too encouraging.

"We all like Dr. Hobson, but his mother is a tartar, and his house is going to be awfully crowded with seven people living in it," Harriet said. "Although at least it means we can stay together."

Christopher resisted the urge to bare his teeth in a growl. "There's nowhere else for you to go?"

He was being shamelessly nosy. Except as Cousin Christopher and the family's landlord, he had an interest beyond mere curiosity in their future. Even if these girls didn't know that.

"We have to split up otherwise, and not to situations where we'll be happy. We're very poor, you see. Uncle Basil gave us a house, but no money, although at least he arranged for the tenants to pay us their rent. But they've had a hard couple of years, too."

Harriet's matter-of-fact tone made Christopher feel even more like a villain in a melodrama. If he had a moustache, he'd be twirling it.

"I'm sorry." In more ways than he could tell his cousins. Even before Basil's death, he'd owed this gallant little family his duty. They were his relatives, after all. Ignorance of their existence was no excuse. He should have made it his business to find out about them.

"So are we," Harriet said, and for a moment, she looked like an adult with adult responsibilities, instead of an adolescent girl.

Christopher felt more like a louse than ever.

He watched Harriet sit up straighter and set her features in a way reminiscent of her half-sister. "We have a great-aunt who lives in Exeter. She's offered to take in Merry and Edwina and me. Or at least pay school fees for Merry and Edwina at some horrid missionary college she donates to."

"What about you?"

Harriet's lips turned down. "Her companion just died. I suspect from overwork. Great-Aunt Dorcas is willing to accept me into her household and train me up to jump to her bidding."

"So you'll be separated from your sisters?" To his regret, he knew Great-Aunt Dorcas. A sourer, more self-righteous, narrowminded, spiteful old biddy didn't exist in England. And that was being generous. Harriet, who he could already tell was a bright, spirited girl, would be buried alive in that gloomy house in Devon.

"Yes. Great-Aunt Dorcas has made it clear that she won't have the girls home for holidays. Nor will she pay me. She says giving me a home fulfills her Christian duty to her nephew's children. I won't be able to travel to see my sisters."

Harriet, who until now hadn't been shy about meeting his eyes, looked away. To his distress, he suspected that she was hiding tears.

"That's cruel."

"And Great-Aunt Dorcas hates Anthea and says she won't lay out a penny to keep her off the streets," Harriet said. "When Great-Aunt Dorcas tried to take us in after Papa's death, Anthea told her to get on her broomstick and fly back to her coven."

Despite this disturbing conversation, that made Christopher laugh. "Good for Anthea."

"She and Winifred are going to go to Winifred's sister in Manchester, but the house is tiny, so they can't stay for long. They both need to earn a living. Winifred's sister is poor, too. Both of them are going to try and find places as governesses, which is so unfair. Winifred should be looking forward to a happy retirement, and Anthea will hate anyone ordering her around."

His short acquaintance with Anthea told Christopher that was true. That was if she managed to find a respectable situation in the first place. No lady in her right mind would take such a beauty into her home.

Even if Anthea found a situation, her looks would make her a target for any unscrupulous males in the vicinity. Worse, she clearly had nobody of influence to look out for her, so she'd be defenseless against any advances.

No wonder Wicked Cousin Christopher came to grief in Edwina's games. His thoughtless instruction to that damn inadequate fool of a lawyer threatened to bring disaster down on this household.

"She will hate that," he said in a grim voice.

"She's trying so hard to be brave and tell us that everything will work out. But we all know that it's just going to be awful." Merry, who he'd already discovered was inclined to be solemn, looked positively tragic.

Not that he could blame her. These children had already seen too much sadness with the loss of their parents. It was clear that the sisters were close. It was also clear that this family had survived and even thrived because of Anthea's love and strength. She wasn't just beautiful. She was a woman of exceptional character.

What she wasn't was a suitable governess.

Christopher hated to admit it, but given the alternatives, marriage to Dr. Hobson emerged as the best choice. Even taking the man's domineering mother into consideration.

Harriet seemed to share his thoughts. "She could marry Dr. Hobson, but she doesn't want to. If she does, it will be because she's trying to keep us together, not because she loves him."

"It's not fair," Merry said. "She's already done so much for us. She shouldn't have to sacrifice the rest of her life to give us a home."

It was true. And Christopher wasn't going to let it happen. He began to think that fate had brought him here at this precise time. If he'd delayed until after Christmas, it would have been too late. The family living at Yardley would be scattered from one end of England to the other. It was possible that he'd never have discovered the wrong he'd committed against his flesh and blood. Not to mention the two women who had cared for his cousins.

He was a rich man. Securing a future for the residents of Yardley Hall would cause him no trouble at all. That deuced presumptuous doctor would have to seek another bride. A conclusion that gave Christopher enormous satisfaction. However unworthy that might be.

As if conjured up by his thoughts, Anthea came through the door, bearing a tray with a teapot and a plate of biscuits. And, he was pleased to see, two cups. That hinted she meant to sit with him for a little while.

She looked tired and harassed, and the unfashionable beige gown didn't flatter her coloring. Why then did Christopher look at her and think she was the prettiest girl he'd ever seen?

"I hope they haven't been pestering you." She sent the two girls a reproving glance. "They've been eaten up with curiosity about you. Your arrival is the most exciting thing that's happened at Yardley in months."

Harriet shot him a glance that told him that she'd rather he didn't reveal the subject of their conversation. But he already knew that Anthea wouldn't approve of the girls confiding in him.

"I haven't been awake long," he said. "They've had a very dull vigil."

"And I'm sure they've been chattering you into the ground since you woke up."

"Lancelot enjoyed talking to us," Merry protested.

"Lancelot?" he echoed in horror.

During his childhood games, neither he nor David had wanted to be the famous knight. The sod was French for a start, and Christopher had grown up when the war was at its height. Not to mention that the brute betrayed his friend Arthur for the sake of getting soppy over Queen Guinevere.

Merry laughed. "You look like we've just given you a dreadful insult."

Harriet was blushing. "We had to call you something, seeing you can't remember your name. Merry said you look like the picture of Lancelot in her book."

"You're much more handsome than Dr. Hobson." Merry picked up the volume from the floor and opened it at a page that showed Lancelot on his knees before Guinevere. The fellow looked like he'd burst into tears if someone said boo.

The picture did nothing to ease Christopher's pique. "The swine looks like he found a worm in his apple."

Anthea laughed, although Harriet was offended. "He's in love. He's beholding the lady he adores."

Merry rolled her eyes, while Christopher scowled at the spineless fop. "I promise you I won't look like that when I'm in love."

"You've both got black hair," Anthea said. "And we needed a name for you, other than 'he who I discovered unconscious in the forest.'"

He continued to survey the picture without pleasure. "You could call me John or Richard or George."

Anthea laughed again. "When you sulk, the resemblance is even stronger."

He humphed with humorous exaggeration.

"We've all sighed over this book in our time," Harriet said.

He humphed again, but he didn't mind. He especially didn't mind, after hearing that the girls considered him handsomer than Dr. Hobson. Although, now he thought about it, he recalled that Merry had said that and not Anthea.

"Girls, I think you've amused our guest for long enough. He's looking tired."

His theatrical scowl deepened. "You don't have to treat me like an invalid."

"But you are an invalid," Merry said with an eight-year-old's tactlessness.

"Which is why I'm sending you two down to help Winifred with the Christmas baking and I'm going to have tea with Lancelot and see if he's feeling any better," Anthea said.

Harriet and Merry obeyed. While Christopher had enjoyed meeting them – and had found the chat devilish interesting – he wasn't sorry when they left him alone with their older sister.

"Would you like some tea?" Anthea asked.

"I'd rather have a brandy." While his incapacitation had its compensations, principally the chance to spend time with his lovely nurse, he didn't much like the menu.

Anthea released a soft huff of laughter. "Dr. Hobson wouldn't approve."

"Plague take Dr. Hobson."

That made her laugh again. "That's not very gracious, when he's ridden through the snow twice to see you. Nor does it do credit to poor Harriet galloping to Shrewsbury to fetch him the day after you arrived."

"He came for your sake, not mine."

That made her blush. "I wondered if you might have been listening. You should have let us know you were awake."

"Instead of shamelessly eavesdropping?"

"Indeed." As he'd known she would, she ignored his request for something more exciting than tea and poured him a cup. "I don't suppose I can rely on you having another lapse of memory."

"I won't mention it, if you don't want me to."

Her lips turned down. "Very diplomatic."

"I thought my silence at the time was rather diplomatic." He accepted the cup and saucer without spilling a drop. That made him ridiculously proud. A sign of just how low he'd sunk over the last few days. The first time she'd handed him a cup, it had felt like a hundredweight.

She poured herself some tea and sat in the chair that Harriet had vacated. Which indicated that she wasn't really angry. "I'm sure curiosity had nothing at all to do with it."

"Perish the thought."

She gave a charming splutter of laughter at his self-righteous tone. He was so besotted with her that everything about her charmed him. Except perhaps her devotion to tea and broth. "I suspect, Mr. Lancelot, that you might be something of a scoundrel."

He grimaced. "I don't see the resemblance."

"The girls meant it as a compliment." She took a sip of tea. "Have you remembered anything?"

He should tell her. It was unconscionable to let her fret, when he'd already decided that he would help this gallant little family. But something in him loved the easy way everyone at Yardley treated him. Was he mistaken to sense a hint of affection? Or was that just wishful thinking?

Most of the world offered him deference and respect, if only because of his wealth and his ancient title. His reception at Yardley consisted of something more sincere and less self-interested.

Right now, Anthea was relaxed in his company. Even if she no longer saw him as Wicked Christopher Trant, once he announced his intention to support the family, the relationship would change from this delightful meeting of equals to gratitude and obligation.

He couldn't bear that. His instincts had been honed in more affairs than a decent man should claim. They insisted that she found him as attractive as he found her. Although the same instincts told him that Anthea was an innocent, for all her undoubted intelligence and competence. She wasn't quite sure what to do with her unfamiliar reaction to the man she'd rescued from the snow.

That was fine with him. When the time was right, he was more than ready to show her.

She was right. He was a scoundrel.

"I remember I don't like tea," he said. "Is there any brandy in the house?"

Sparkling blue eyes leveled on him and punched the breath from his lungs. By God, she was a glorious woman. It was a travesty that she was stuck here, harried with household duties and with just a provincial hobbledehoy of a doctor to dazzle.

"We keep a bottle in the kitchen for medicinal purposes and for cooking. Unless Winifred used it all in the Christmas pudding."

"Will you check for me?"

"I most certainly will not. Your wits are addled enough without adding strong spirits into the mix."

"Cruel mistress."

Her cheeks were rosy, and the hand that lifted her cup was unsteady. She was adorably ruffled. Telling her his true identity would raise barriers between them, just when he read unmistakable signs that he'd found a chink in her armor.

He'd tell her tomorrow that he'd recovered his memory.

Maybe.

"Would you prefer coffee to tea?" He could tell that she made a major effort to keep her voice steady.

Actually, he'd prefer kisses to tea or coffee. Or even brandy. But it was too early to press her. He was well aware that if he made Anthea too uncomfortable, Winifred would take over the nursing.

"For breakfast? Yes, I would. Thank you."

"I'll see what I can do."

"Perhaps I could come downstairs tomorrow. I'm getting deuced tired of this nightshirt." It was so voluminous that it tangled about him whenever he moved.

"It was my stepfather's. He got very stout before he died. We managed to rescue your clothes, you'll be pleased to know."

"So I can get out of bed?"

"Dr. Hobson said—"

"Damn Dr. Hobson." He paused. "He's not good enough for you, you know."

Her eyes narrowed, and she placed the cup on the saucer with an audible click. "You said you wouldn't mention it."

"I forgot. You know I'm having problems with my memory." He gave an exaggerated grimace and extended his cup and saucer, trying to look as harmless as a duckling. "More tea?"

CHAPTER SIX

*W*hen Anthea carried in her patient's breakfast the next morning, he was still asleep. Trying to be quiet, she slid the tray onto the chest of drawers and indulged in a moment to study him. Yesterday, she'd dug out her stepfather's shaving kit for him, although Winifred had insisted on supervising the actual shave. Now Lancelot looked less like a dashing bewhiskered pirate, and more like his namesake in Merry's book.

It was something of a relief not to have those glittering golden eyes fixed on her. When he looked at her as if she made all his prayers come true, her traitorous heart performed all sorts of contortions and she had difficulty breathing. She tried to tell herself that he was a stranger who would disappear from her life as suddenly as he'd crashed into it. But every time she saw that highbred face with its cynical expression and sensual lips, she couldn't stop herself from longing for things that she could never have.

It was so cursed unfair that fate placed such temptation before her, just when her choices narrowed down to doing her duty by her sisters. How could she say no to marrying Philip? She couldn't let

Harriet become Great-Aunt Dorcas's domestic drudge, and the idea of her two younger sisters caged in that horrid, spartan school was unbearable.

Philip was a good man, and he said he loved her. Not only that, he was considered a catch in the county. Handsome. Clever. Prosperous. Urbane.

Anthea liked him, although she'd noted his occasional pomposity. What was that weighed against his kind nature? She should be on her knees in gratitude that such a paragon was willing to take her on. Not just her. Her sisters and Winifred as well.

Philip offered her a future and a home of her own, even if one ruled by his harridan of a mother. Why on earth was she hesitating?

Except that she'd so wanted to fall in love with the man she chose to wed. And some deep-rooted instinct warned her that it was wrong to accept another man's proposal while she remained in thrall to the mysterious Lancelot.

Which was mad when she knew nothing about him. Not even his real name. As Winifred said, he could be a man of bad character. Even worse in her view, much as she might blush to admit it, he could be married or committed elsewhere.

One thing she was sure of was that Lancelot liked her. Despite being unfamiliar with flirtation, she knew that he found her attractive. At least he always brightened up whenever she appeared, and she couldn't mistake the glint of male interest in his gaze when he looked at her.

But she had a suspicion that this was a man with an eye for a pretty woman and his reaction was no more than a natural masculine appreciation for the opposite sex. He must be bored to death, confined in bed as he was. If he flirted with his nurse, it was no more than a way to pass the time. He was worldly and sophisticated, and women must fawn over him wherever he went. Even if he thought of Anthea as more than brief entertainment in a tedious day, he could look higher than an impoverished woman past first youth for any more permanent association.

Which made her want to gnash her teeth and throw a fit, however out of character that was. She'd done her best to accept her lot in life, but when she looked at naughty, beautiful, alluring Lancelot, forbidden yearnings made her rail against her cloistered existence.

Innocent she might be. A fool she was not. She could tell that this was a man who had committed a thousand sins, even if right now he couldn't recall them. She had no doubt that if she was willing to forsake her virtue, he'd be happy to sin with her. The thought was fiercely appealing, but she had too many responsibilities to conduct a short-term affair with a beguiling stranger.

More was the pity.

He stirred. Those almost feminine lashes, so incongruent in that arrogant, masculine face, flickered and Anthea found herself under that quizzical regard once more. Her idiotic heart cramped with longing. Just once, she'd like her days to be packed full of excitement. Just once, she'd love to be free to express her deepest desires.

Meeting Lancelot was the most exciting thing that had ever happened to her. She was close to twenty-six, and her life had been all toil and obligation. Anthea couldn't help feeling that her youth was passing her by. She'd reach a blameless old age with nothing thrilling to remember at all.

What a tragedy.

The inevitable price of surrendering to Lancelot would be heartache. But every feminine instinct told her that the pleasure might be worth it.

"Good morning, Anthea," he said drowsily, a slow smile curving his lips.

She couldn't mistake his pleasure in seeing her. As if she arrived accompanied by trumpets and choirs singing hallelujah. Her sisters loved her, she knew, but they often took her for granted. It was cursed addictive to have this handsome devil greet her as though she turned his winter into bright summer.

"Good morning, Lancelot," she said and laughed when he rolled his eyes.

He pushed up against the pillows and the nightshirt gaped over his bare chest, revealing crisp dark curls on a hard, muscled chest. Her hands curled at her sides, as she fought the urge to reach out and touch that golden skin under the light covering of hair.

If only she felt like this when she looked at Philip, she thought in despair. But while the idea of Lancelot placing his long-fingered hands on her body made her feel like she'd swallowed fire, the prospect of Philip touching her aroused only a vague distaste.

Heaven help her. She was doomed whatever she did.

"I hope you brought me a nice rare sirloin."

"Oh, two." To hide this man's powerful effect on her, she turned to pick up the tray. There was something so breathtakingly intimate in watching him wake up. She could be a lover or a wife, rather than a nurse and a stranger.

"It's porridge again, isn't it?" he asked in a long-suffering tone.

"It is." She set the tray on his lap and stepped out of reach. Goodness, it wasn't even eight o'clock in the morning. She should be thinking wholesome thoughts, not seduction. "But I did make you coffee."

"Thank you." It was odd. When she'd discovered him in the snow, she'd decided that he was the rudest man she'd ever met. Yet it turned out that he had excellent manners.

"Would you like me to pour it?"

"Yes, please."

That was a pity. It meant that she had to venture closer once more. In the confined space, she was too aware of the clean scent of his skin. Soap and something tangy that she'd recognize in a crowd of a hundred people.

That scent wove its way through her dreams. She already knew that it would haunt her after he left.

Because he would leave. His memory would come back, or someone would arrive looking for him. Men like him didn't belong at ramshackle Yardley Hall.

Nor as it turned out did she, thanks to Lord Denton. While Lancelot would no doubt return to a life overflowing with enjoyment and adventure, she was doomed to an unappealing marriage or a post as a downtrodden governess. It was enough to make her want to tear her hair and stamp her feet.

Anthea poured his coffee and passed it across. As he took the saucer, their fingers brushed. A searing tingle of heat made her gasp and jerk back. Thank goodness he was steadier than he'd been a couple of days ago, or coffee would have spilled all over the bedding.

Something in his eyes changed. She might be the only game on offer, but it was clear that he was vitally interested in playing.

Not that she could do a thing about that, with three young girls and Winifred in the house. She'd already admitted that morality exerted no pull over what she wished to do with this man. For a quarter of a century, she'd lived as pure as the snow that surrounded the house. To her shame, she knew that if Lancelot touched her, she couldn't rely on native virtue to keep her safe.

"Anthea?"

Just one word. Her name.

That deep voice made her shiver to the bone with an awareness that she didn't want to feel but she couldn't combat. "Yes?"

Perhaps it was lucky that Winifred breezed in at that moment, carrying a folded pile of Lancelot's clothes. "Good morning," she said, then paused in the doorway with a troubled expression on her lined face.

Anthea blushed, although she was several feet away from the bed and Lancelot hadn't moved any closer. But Winifred knew her too well, and Anthea feared that lust was written all over her face. Trying to hide her shaking hands, she began to clear away the glasses and water jug from the chest of drawers.

"Good morning, Miss French," Lancelot said with a debonair smoothness that told Anthea he was no beginner when it came to hiding his reaction to a woman he wanted. Because he did want her. When their hands touched, she'd read a lust in his eyes to equal hers. "How are you this morning?"

"Wide awake to any tricks you might play, my fine young buck."

He laughed as if Winifred was joking, but Anthea heard the warning that underlay her governess's words. "No tricks from me."

"So you say. Are you ready to tell us who you are yet?"

"No, still in the dark."

He sounded remarkably cheerful about the matter, Anthea couldn't help noting. She picked up a glass half-full of water but fumbled it. "Blast."

The tray of glassware on the chest was now awash.

"Are you all right, Annie?" Winifred asked.

She wasn't. She feared that she'd never be all right again. How could she be, when what she wanted was all so wrong?

Anthea came late to discovering the power of physical attraction. She felt helpless against its demands. So cruel to learn how it felt to want a man, just as she was on the verge of giving herself to a man she didn't want at all.

"I'll get a towel," she mumbled. Avoiding Winifred's curiosity, she crossed to the washstand behind the screen.

"Are those for me?" Lancelot asked Winifred, as Anthea mopped up the mess.

"I thought you might like to get dressed and come downstairs. You must be sick of being stuck in bed."

"I am indeed."

"And it will save us having to lug your meals up to you. My old knees will appreciate the break."

"He shouldn't overdo things." Anthea had regained enough composure to sound like her usual self. "He's still not well."

Oh, what a miserable sinner she was to try and keep him in this bedroom. It was clear that Winifred was trying to stop her from being alone with Lancelot. A proper young lady would appreciate the reprieve.

It was clear that she wasn't a proper young lady.

She'd loved having him to herself, drinking in the sight of him and imagining his kisses. Not only that, she'd also lose the private pleasure of his conversation. There had been such joy in talking to someone her own age. Someone clever and funny and interested. Someone who could be friend as well as lover, if circumstances were different.

"He doesn't have to stay downstairs all day," Winifred said repressively.

Lancelot picked up his spoon and attacked his porridge with a readiness that contradicted his complaints. "I'll be glad to get out of this nightshirt."

"I'll leave your clothes here, then," Winifred said with an edge to her voice. "Annie, the girls are waiting to have breakfast with you."

"Yes, Winifred," she said in a subdued voice.

Her friend acted in her best interests. She shouldn't want to throw her out of the window into the snow.

"So I'm to languish all alone?" Lancelot asked with theatrical gloominess.

Winifred shot him a darkling look. "Use the time to contemplate your misdeeds."

He gave a short huff of laughter. "However legion they may be, I don't remember them."

Winifred didn't smile. "I'm sure you'll come up with a few that you've committed in the last few days. Anthea?"

Anthea dropped the wet towel on the tray and curled her hands around the handles. "I'll come up to get your breakfast things later."

"I'm sure he can bring them down himself," Winifred said in an uncompromising tone. "There doesn't look like there's much wrong with him to me."

"But he doesn't know where to go," Anthea said.

"He'll find his way. The house isn't that big. Apart from not knowing who he is, he seems in perfect health. Now he's no longer bedridden, it's unsuitable for you to be in here on your own, my girl."

Anthea bent her head without replying. It was absurd, but this denial of Lancelot's company made her want to cry.

Although Winifred was right. She shouldn't be making regular visits to a man's sleeping chamber. There was nobody to gossip about her improper behavior, but gossip wasn't the only danger he presented.

Hadn't she been about to beg him to touch her this morning? And it was apparent that with the slightest encouragement, he'd leap to explore the attraction flaring between them.

Winifred continued to give instructions to Lancelot. "I brought up some hot water before you woke up, so you should be ready to get your day underway."

"Aye–aye, Captain," he said.

Despite the ache in her heart, that gave Anthea a smile. He didn't make Winifred smile. "You won't charm me, young sir. I've seen a thousand bright-eyed popinjays like you in my time, and nine hundred and ninety-nine better."

That made him laugh, which reminded Anthea that her conversations with him were the only touch of lightness in the last grim months. Winifred was right to step in to restore the proprieties, but that didn't stop her interference from rankling.

Without looking at Lancelot, Anthea made her way onto the landing. But she wasn't quick enough to escape.

"What on earth is going on, Anthea?" Winifred asked in a fierce whisper, following her out.

"Nothing," she said sullenly.

"Make sure it stays that way. That young devil has his eye on you. And I don't like it."

"I haven't done anything wrong. Nor has he."

"You could cut the air with a knife when I came in. I don't want you alone with him anymore. He's no longer an invalid. If he decides to take advantage of you, you won't have a hope of fighting him off."

The brazen stranger inside her thrilled to think of Lancelot taking liberties. Heaven forgive her, but she wouldn't do much fighting. Even worse, she feared that Winifred knew it. "He's been a perfect gentleman."

"So far. Nonetheless, I'll look after him from now on."

"What about your knees?"

"Better my knees complain a bit than that you find yourself compromised, my girl. Things are bad enough at Yardley, without you giving up your maidenhead to the first handsome rogue who takes your fancy."

"Winifred, that's enough," she said, although Winifred only gave blunt expression to ideas that had already lodged in her mind.

"All right. I'll hold my peace, as long as you show me that you're not about to do something stupid. I'm surprised at you, Annie. You need to set an example for the girls."

"You don't need to say any more," Anthea said through tight lips.

"Once I'd never have had to say anything." Winifred scowled at her. "You've always had your head screwed on. I'm not sure I recognize you now."

Anthea kept her voice low, well aware that Lancelot had sharp ears and that he wasn't above eavesdropping. "A little flirtation with a charming stranger isn't a deadly sin. I know what I owe my sisters. I know what I owe my good name. You don't need to lecture me. I haven't done anything beyond what I've needed to do to nurse him back to health."

Winifred pursed her lips. "Don't try and pull the wool over my eyes, young lady. I've seen the way you look at each other."

"Looking won't do me any harm."

"It's what looking might lead to that I'm afraid of. I never thought I'd say this, but the sooner we're all out of Yardley Hall, the better."

Anthea adjusted the tray which, while not heavy, was awkward. "Winifred, you don't mean that."

"Yes, I do." Her old governess crossed her arms and surveyed her with displeasure. "I want you well away from that silver-tongued miscreant before you do something that you'll live to regret."

All the fight rushed out of Anthea, as she gave a heavy sigh. "He makes me feel alive."

"I'm sure, but you have people who depend on you. You have a future to prepare for."

"I know," she said in a bleak voice. "But it's not a future I want."

Winifred looked stricken and reached out for her arm. "Oh, my dear."

Anthea stepped back to avoid the sympathetic gesture. Over the last week, she'd felt like she was about to shatter under the pressure of her responsibilities. If she unbent enough to let Winifred hug her, she feared that she'd start to cry and she wouldn't stop.

"I know my duty and I'll do it. Don't worry, Winifred. Nothing dire will happen. We can't leave the hall now, in any case. Lancelot doesn't know who he is. Even if he did, the snow has closed all the roads. Let's do our best to give the girls one last Christmas at Yardley to remember. Then if Lancelot's memory hasn't returned, he can take lodgings with Dr. Hobson. You and I will move in with your sister, and the girls will go to Great-Aunt Dorcas."

Winifred looked even more concerned. "So you're not going to marry Dr. Hobson?"

"How can I, when I want another man?"

"How can you not, when he's offered all of us a home?"

"But he thinks that I'll come to love him," she said in despair. "If I marry him now, it would be a lie."

"Annie, you're not..."

Not in love with Lancelot? Winifred couldn't even say the words. "Don't ask, Winifred. I don't know the answer. I don't want to know the answer."

Winifred's compassion stung more than her criticism. Unable to bear any more, Anthea turned and trudged downstairs, her heart as heavy as an anvil.

CHAPTER SEVEN

knock at the door made Christopher's heart rise in hope. Had Anthea decided to defy Winifred's dictates and come to him anyway? When the women had left the room, he'd heard some heated whispers from the hallway outside, but he hadn't been able to make out what was said.

He couldn't blame Winifred for putting her foot down about Anthea wandering in and out of his bedroom without a hint of a chaperone. Much as he regretted the edict. When the older woman had turned up, he'd been on the verge of dragging the girl down for a kiss. The heat in Anthea's eyes had told him that she wouldn't put up any opposition.

With him in bed and wearing only a threadbare nightshirt, who knew where that kiss might have led? Anthea's virtue had been in immediate danger, once the polite mask crumbled and desire ignited between them.

Now he was dressed in his own clothes at last, and he'd shaved and washed and combed his hair. He felt much more like dashing Lord Denton than a helpless invalid.

"Come in," he said, turning away from the window. Not that there was much to see outside apart from endless snow.

"Mr. Lancelot, would you like to come downstairs and help us put up the Christmas greenery?" No surprise, although a disappointment to see Merry and Harriet in the doorway.

"I'd be delighted," he said in answer to Harriet's invitation.

"Oh, topping," Merry said. "You're so tall, it will save us having to get up on the ladder all the time."

That made him laugh. "So you're just out to take shameless advantage of me, you abominable child?"

He liked these girls and was proud to call them his cousins. He even liked Winifred, much as her supervision galled him. It was clear that she loved her charges. Nor did she hesitate to speak her mind without fear or favor.

"Merry, that wasn't nice," Harriet said.

"But it's true. You don't mind helping, do you, Mr. Lancelot?"

"If it gets me out of this room, I'm happy to do anything. Even stretch up to pin a bit of holly to the wall."

"And mistletoe. We've got a lot of mistletoe this year," Merry said with an enthusiasm he hadn't seen in her before. "We were lucky there was plenty close to the house. It started snowing again before we could go too far out."

He gave them a theatrical leer. "Does that mean I can claim a kiss from my lovely hostesses?"

Harriet blushed. "It would be rude not to, although Anthea told us we had to be gentle with you, because it's your first day out of bed."

The idea of Anthea being gentle with him made his blood simmer. Not to mention the opportunities for mischief that a bumper crop of mistletoe presented. He could hardly wait. "Lead the way, girls."

As Harriet collected his breakfast tray, he picked up the pail of water from his morning ablutions. It was a shock quite how heavy the bucket felt. He was disgusted at his lingering weakness.

As they made their way down to the kitchens, he took in the details of the manor. He saw more of what he already knew. The house's interior was well maintained but undeniably worn and in need of new paint and fabrics. The main staircase was elegant, and the hall had graceful proportions. Tall mullioned windows let in stark gray winter light, and a fire blazed in a large hearth. Despite the shabbiness, it was a congenial space. There was love in this house. He could feel it.

Near the door, he noticed piles of branches. The scent of freshly cut pine added a pleasant tang to the air. He hadn't given much thought to how close it was to Christmas. Once he became an adult, the day had lost its magic. Now something young and optimistic inside him, silent since his boyhood, stirred happy expectations.

Who knew what this Christmas might bring?

He crossed the parquetry floor before following a corridor to a cavernous old-fashioned kitchen, where Edwina sat drawing at a large oak table, Winifred stirred something over a range, and Anthea stood at the sink, washing up.

It was a scene of cozy domesticity, more suited to a room packed with servants than to the ladies of the house. He'd already noticed that the sisters insisted on very little ceremony.

All three occupants of the kitchen looked up at his entrance and regarded him with various degrees of welcome. Winifred displayed the usual wariness.

Anthea smiled with unalloyed pleasure, then clearly thought better of it. Edwina squealed with excitement and jumped off her chair to run toward him. He couldn't help thinking that once she discovered that he was Wicked Cousin Christopher, she mightn't be quite so glad to see him.

"Mr. Lancelot! I've got some mistletoe. Will you kiss me?"

He laughed and went down on his haunches. "I'd consider it a privilege, Edwina."

The girl fished a bruised sprig of greenery out of her pocket and held it over his head. "We never have anyone new to play with at Christmas. It's nice to get someone different to kiss."

"I couldn't agree more," he said in a solemn voice.

He heard Anthea's splutter of laughter, and he ignored Winifred's narrow-eyed glare.

Edwina closed her eyes and tilted her chin. "I'm ready."

For a homicidal maniac, she was adorable. Taking a second, Christopher stared at this child and realized that somewhere during the last few days, he'd developed a genuine fondness for his cousins. He bent and pressed a kiss to Edwina's forehead with a poignant emotion that he hadn't expected to feel.

"There," he said softly, as the girl's eyes opened. Her beatific smile squeezed his once invulnerable heart. "Now I'll kiss you."

Christopher caught Anthea watching him with an arrested expression. He sent her a faint smile. "Lucky me."

Edwina seized him by the shoulders and placed a smacking kiss on his cheek.

"I'm overcome," he said, pretending to lose his balance. As he straightened, he placed a hand over where Edwina had kissed him. "I'll never wash that cheek again."

Which made Edwina giggle. "You're silly."

"Mr. Lancelot, will you kiss me next?" Merry asked, rushing up to stand beside Edwina.

He rose to his feet, chagrined at the effort it cost him. "I need to cook some more kisses first," he said, which made the two girls laugh.

"Cook one for me, too, please," Harriet said. "Why should my sisters have all the fun?"

"You're definitely on my list," he said with a growl that had Harriet giggling, too.

"And Anthea and Winifred," Edwina said, jumping up and down at his side to gain his attention. "You'll have to kiss them, as well."

"Give the poor man some peace," Anthea said, although she didn't sound like she minded too much. "He'll have to go back to bed at this rate."

If it meant going to bed with Anthea, he approved of the idea, but he merely said, "I've seen quite enough of that bed for the moment, thank you."

He stepped forward and picked up a cloth to dry the crockery draining on the sink. Anthea cast him a startled look and dropped the plate she was washing with a splash.

"Do you know what you're doing with that towel, sir?" Winifred asked in an unimpressed tone.

"I'm sure I can work it out," he said lightly.

The younger girls stared at him with wide eyes. "Haven't you ever dried a dish before, Lancelot?" Harriet asked in the same tone that she'd use if he'd sprouted wings and flown up to the ceiling.

"Perhaps I've forgotten."

"No, you said you remembered all the normal things like how to clean your teeth, or do up your buttons."

"My goodness, you must be very rich," Merry said in awe.

He was. So rich that he felt a pang of guilt about how privileged he'd been.

"Have you been in a kitchen before?" Anthea asked with a hint of irony.

"I'm sure I must have been," he said and noticed Winifred's frown. He supposed that she dismissed him as a useless layabout. Right now, he was inclined to agree with her.

"Probably to make a nuisance of yourself instead of doing anything helpful," she said with a sniff.

He wanted to protest. Although the sad truth was that Winifred was right. As a boy, he'd hung around the kitchens in hope of cadging a treat from the cook, and he'd often raided the larder when he was hungry after midnight and he was supposed to be in bed.

As an adult, he couldn't remember setting foot in his kitchens, either at Meadowbank, his mansion in Surrey, or at his Mayfair residence, Trant House. These days, if he was hungry after hours, he just needed to request a snack from his attentive staff.

Glancing around the cheerful room on this gray morning, he couldn't help but feel that he'd missed out on a treat. The atmosphere was delightfully familial. He'd already remarked on the love that he sensed in this house. It seemed concentrated in this warm space, with everybody busy doing something useful and the smell of good food in the air.

Christopher placed a dry plate on the bench and picked up another and told himself that it was ridiculous to feel a sense of achievement.

"Should I take over?" Harriet said. "You're a guest, after all."

"An uninvited one," he said, finishing with that plate and lifting the next. There was something rather soothing about finding his rhythm as a kitchen helper. "I need to repay your kindness."

"If you spend the day fending off my sisters' attempts to trap you under the mistletoe, you'll have more than enough to keep you occupied," Anthea said, setting another clean plate on the drainer.

He cast her a searching glance, as he started to dry it. "Only your sisters?"

Faint color in her cheeks told him that she knew what he was asking. She kept her profile to him. It was clear that the charged moment between them in his bedroom this morning left her feeling awkward in his company. "Well, there's Winifred."

"There is."

"I'm too old to put up with any of your nonsense." With an audible clang, the woman placed the lid on the fragrant stew that she'd been stirring.

"That's a pity. I'll have to sneak up on you before you can avoid me," he said. "You know it's bad luck to refuse a kiss under the mistletoe, don't you?"

"It means that you won't get married for a year," Merry said solemnly. "Although the tradition of kissing goes back to the Druids, who believed the plant was sacred."

"I have no wish to get married next year. Any year, in fact," Winifred said with a hint of asperity. "Men are more trouble than they're worth in my opinion."

"Harsh," he said without resentment. "I can see I won't persuade Miss French to kiss me. What about you, Anthea?"

"I'm with Winifred on this," she said, staring down at the pottery bowl she was washing as if it concealed the secrets of the ages. He'd never seen her so skittish. "And I don't care if I don't get married next year either."

Christopher bit back a question about Dr. Hobson. He didn't want to remind her of her suitor. Which begged the question of whether he counted himself as a suitor, too.

"Someone else for me to sneak up on, then," he said, and endured a reproving stare from sapphire eyes as he picked up the bowl and began to wipe it.

They started putting up the Christmas greenery in the hall before moving on to an attractive drawing room with views over snowy lawns. The weather was closing in, which Christopher didn't mind at all. Right now, he had no wish to go anywhere else. Although he continued to hope that his horse had found a stable somewhere.

The house was old and unpretentious and considerably smaller than his other properties. Meadowbank was a vast edifice, built last century in the Palladian style and full of echoing rooms. It made a suitable official residence for the influential Earls of Denton, but nobody would ever describe it as cozy.

Yardley was much older and more like a family home. He found himself charmed by its Elizabethan details, like the linenfold paneling and mullioned windows.

"Don't overdo it," Anthea said, joining him as he watched Merry tie bunches of mistletoe together with scarlet ribbon.

At first, Anthea had kept her distance, but with all the outrageous teasing and silly jokes and the fact that Edwina and Merry needed help to play their part in the decorating, she'd lost her self-consciousness. By now, she treated him with the casual friendliness that he'd so enjoyed when bedridden.

"I'm fine," he said.

"You're not really."

He wasn't really. So when she collapsed onto the window seat behind her, he was very pleased to sit next to her. When he'd come downstairs this morning, he'd felt almost back to his old self. A day of lifting and bending and stretching left him feeling like he was made of wet string.

He watched Harriet lift Edwina up to pin more mistletoe to the colored paper chains draped over the next window. "They've got endless energy, haven't they?"

"They love Christmas. Having another person to play with is an extra treat."

He waited for her to say something about it being their last Christmas at Yardley, but there seemed to be an unspoken agreement that only cheerful subjects were acceptable today. "They're lovely girls. And a credit to you."

Anthea sent him a quick smile. "I don't think I did much. If anyone deserves praise, it's Winifred."

Winifred who came through the door, bearing a laden tray. They'd stopped for lunch, but it was now after four, and the short day drew to a close. Outside, it was cold and icy. In this room, all was affection and laughter and a blazing fire in the hearth and the sharp, clean smell of winter greenery.

As Winifred dispensed elderflower cordial to the girls, Christopher looked around the greenery-bedecked drawing room and experienced an unfamiliar emotion. It felt very much like contentment. Or at least, he supposed it was.

He'd known plenty of excitement and passion. But he couldn't remember a time when he'd sat back, satisfied to be where he was and in his present company. Even the knowledge that he had to tell these people who he was – and soon – wasn't enough to pierce his well-being.

Winifred offered cups of mulled wine to Christopher and Anthea. "Are you talking about me behind my back?"

Anthea took a cup and smiled at the older woman. "Only in the most glowing of terms."

Christopher picked up a cup and lifted it in a silent toast. "We wouldn't be game to say anything else."

"Just as it should be." Winifred set the tray on a graceful mahogany table and started to carry plates of mince pies and fruitcake around the room.

"I don't know what I'd have done without her since Mamma died," Anthea said. "The girls were so young when I had to take charge. Edwina wasn't much more than a baby. Even Harriet was only ten."

"It's a lonely life you lead here," he said softly. "You should be dancing every night and flirting with an army of admirers."

She gave a dismissive laugh. "That sounds like more hard work than bringing up the girls. Although we're not altogether isolated. We often dine with the neighbours, when the weather doesn't trap us in this valley, and there are occasional assemblies in Shrewsbury. Anyway, my life at Yardley hasn't been all bad. Most of it has been good, in fact. At least I've had nobody to order me around."

"Except Winifred."

Anthea took a sip of her wine. "Her bark is worse than her bite."

"I suspect she'd bite like the devil himself, if she thought someone threatened the people she loves."

"Yes, she's loyal. She'd never have stayed with us otherwise. I wish..."

Christopher waited to hear Anthea express regret for the fate awaiting them. Instead, she straightened. "I'm sorry you're not with people you love at this time of year. It must be difficult to be among strangers."

"You and the girls don't feel like strangers," he said, meaning it.

His mother's cronies infested his usual Christmas. Of course, he was happy to see his brother and he loved his dear mamma, even if she drove him to distraction. He'd particularly liked the years when his cousin Grayson Maddox, Lord Halston, joined the celebrations. Gray had married last year, and he and his new wife were now busy establishing their own family traditions.

But the holiday season at Morton House lacked the warmth he felt at Yardley, and he found that he didn't at all miss the ostentatious festivities.

"You're very good with the girls." Anthea cast him a thoughtful glance. "It makes me wonder if you have children of your own."

"I'm sure I don't." Good God, no. In fact, until he'd come to Yardley, he'd never shown much interest in other people's offspring. Perhaps he felt an affinity with Anthea's sisters because they were his cousins. Or perhaps he just liked them because they displayed more distinct personalities than most of the children he'd come across.

"But how can you be sure?" She frowned. "You don't even know your name."

It was way past time that he stopped pretending to be a passing traveler with no link to Yardley. Anthea needed to know that if he expressed an interest, it wasn't as a cheating husband to some other mythical lady.

He braced to tell her the truth, praying that it wouldn't shred the friendship built up over the last days.

Only now, when he readied himself to expose his true identity, did he admit quite how much Anthea's good opinion mattered. If she decided that she couldn't forgive Wicked Cousin Christopher for his carelessness, he'd be devastated.

"Anthea—"

"You promised me a kiss, Mr. Lancelot," Merry said, rushing across and holding one of her mistletoe garlands over his head.

He laughed, ashamed to acknowledge his relief at not having to confess who he was. Anyway, surely he was better to tell Anthea when they were alone, and she could decide how best to share the news with the rest of her family.

"I did." He stood up and took the sprig from her, holding it over her head. "Close your eyes."

"Why?"

"Because it's tradition."

Obediently, she shut her eyes and angled her face up. He bent and pressed a gentle kiss to her forehead.

She opened her eyes and giggled in a very un-Meredith Garland kind of way. "That was nice."

"It was. Wishing you the very best of the season, Merry."

She smiled at him with an open affection that chipped yet another corner off his cynical heart. By heaven, if he stayed here much longer, his hard-living London friends wouldn't recognize him.

"And to you, Mr. Lancelot."

"My turn." Harriet stepped up.

"Lucky me," Christopher said. "Having the prettiest girls in England lining up for a kiss."

"You have to close your eyes, Harriet," Merry said, as if she communicated a royal edict.

Christopher suspended the mistletoe over the girl's head and bent to kiss her cheek. Whatever the outcome of his adventures in Shropshire, he was very glad to have made his cousins' acquaintance. They were all grand girls.

Harriet sighed and opened her eyes. "Merry's right. That *was* nice."

Winifred stood by the fireplace, watching them with an unreadable expression. He waggled the mistletoe. "What about you, Miss French? I'm giving away kisses for free."

"I'm sure not for the first time," she said with a hint of sourness.

"That just means I'm very good at kissing."

His teasing deepened Winifred's frown. "You won't be practicing on me, you young rascal. I've got work to do. Dinner won't cook itself." She picked up the tray and stomped out of the room, the rigidity of her back eloquent of her disdain for such frivolity.

Christopher shrugged and turned toward Anthea, who sat on the window seat watching the antics with bright, laughing eyes. "Now it's your turn, Anthea."

He'd planned on kissing Anthea since Edwina had produced that ragged shred of mistletoe this morning in the kitchen.

"No, thank you," she said, going as red as a rose.

"Anthea, you have to play." Edwina joined her sisters. "It's Christmas."

Anthea's lips pursed in disagreement. He knew that she did it to indicate disapproval, but the result made her lush pink mouth look even more kissable than ever. Winifred had responded with similar derision, but the effect was quite different coming from a beautiful girl. Christopher suffered a jolt of arousal at the thought of touching his mouth to hers.

"It's not Christmas yet," Anthea said.

"But it's nearly Christmas," Merry said. "It's Christmas Eve tomorrow."

"Imagine if some handsome prince comes riding up the driveway and falls madly in love with you," Harriet said. "Then you find the mistletoe has cursed your hopes."

That made Anthea laugh. "I'll take my chances. The only thing likely to come galloping up to Yardley through all this snow is a hungry polar bear."

"No kisses?" Christopher asked, not having to pretend disappointment, even if he couldn't kiss Anthea now the way that he wanted to. Not with three pairs of curious eyes watching on.

He ached for some physical contact. When he'd arrived, she'd touched him over and over to help him sit up or to make him more comfortable in bed or to pass him something that he needed. Since his strength had revived, she'd kept her distance. It was enough to make a healthy man want to be incapacitated again.

He'd hoped that when they did the decorating, he'd need to hoist her up or assist her down from a ladder or a chair. Instead, she'd designated him as the younger girls' helper and spent most of her time supervising from floor level.

"You've had three kisses today. That should keep you going for the moment."

The problem was that as his vigor returned, so did his predatory instincts. He rapidly came to the conclusion that he wouldn't be satisfied until he had Anthea under him in a bed.

He couldn't seduce her. Even if she knew who he was – and he was sure she wouldn't like him once she did – there were a hundred other reasons why he couldn't have her. He owed her his gratitude for saving his life. She was a chaste gentlewoman who deserved his respect. She had nobody to protect her. If he led her astray, he was no better than the men she was likely to fall foul of if she became a governess. Moreover, he couldn't shame her in front of her sisters, his kinswomen.

So many reasons to stay away from Anthea.

Ranged against that was a voracious hunger, stronger than he'd ever known. The unwelcome reality was he wasn't sure that his principles would prevail against the inescapable fact that he wanted her.

So it was a struggle to sound as if her refusal didn't strike a blow to his desires, however discreditable. Yet he managed it. "When you say for the moment, does that mean you might kiss me later?"

"Go on, Anthea," Edwina said, jumping up and down. "He's kissed everyone else."

"He hasn't kissed Winifred," she said.

"I'll catch her, too," he said. "I can run faster than she can."

"Everyone can run faster than she can," Merry said, rolling her eyes.

"Can you run faster than me?" Christopher asked Merry.

"I don't know. I don't think so." She directed a measuring look at him. "We can have a race in the hall to find out."

"No, you jolly well can't," Anthea said, laughing. "Give Mr. Lancelot some breathing space. You three dreadful girls have been at him all day, and he's just out of his sickbed."

"Do you mind, Mr. Lancelot?" Harriet asked.

"If I did, would I kiss you all under the mistletoe?"

"See, Anthea?" Merry said. "He likes us."

Anthea sighed. "Goodness knows why. Now it's time you all started your evening chores and you give Mr. Lancelot some peace."

In a giggling pack, the girls left Christopher on his own with Anthea. He stood up and extended his hand. "Alone at last."

Her lips flattened. "I'm not going to kiss you. I'm too old for ridiculous games."

He smiled down at her, delighted and frustrated in equal measure. "Just old enough, I'd say."

She subjected him to a searching regard. "I think you're a bit of a rogue, sir."

"Only a bit?"

To his pleasure, she laughed and allowed him to help her to her feet. "I was being polite."

CHAPTER EIGHT

nthea lay wakeful in her bed and stared into the thick darkness. Tomorrow was Christmas Eve. She could probably keep the family at Yardley until after New Year, given the snowy conditions. After that, they'd have to leave.

Also looming was Boxing Day, when she had to give Dr. Hobson an answer to his proposal. Common sense told her that marrying the prosperous doctor would solve a lot of problems. It was unfortunate that she had no real connection with him. Perhaps that mightn't be enough to deter her from a course that offered so many advantages. But how could she promise herself to a fine man who took her in good faith, when her interest was fixed elsewhere?

On the other hand, how could she deny Harriet, Merry, and Edwina a chance for a home? How could she send Winifred out to work with strangers at her age?

These problems had kept her awake for weeks, although the addition of Lancelot into the mix had complicated everything. Her choices would be easier, if no more appealing, if she'd never stumbled across a handsome gentleman in the snow.

But how could she regret these last few days? Most of all today, which had been one of the happiest that she'd ever spent.

For a short interval, her difficulties had receded and she'd tasted genuine joy. The girls had been their old spirited selves, and Anthea had laughed with a wholehearted appreciation that she couldn't remember feeling since the news of Sir Basil's death.

While she'd tried to keep her head through all the fun and merriment, it had been impossible. Because Lancelot was right. Despite her love for her sisters and her friendship with Winifred, this was a lonely life. When her mother was alive, she'd had someone to share her burdens, but for the last five years, she'd been alone in so many ways. As she'd told Lancelot, she'd had no chance to enjoy the carefree pastimes of youth. No London season or flirtations or secret kisses.

So there had been a giddy pleasure today, sharing the company of an attractive man who treated her as if she thrilled him as much as he thrilled her. Every glance, every word had carried an undercurrent of unspoken craving that transformed the day to magic.

Dangerous magic. Although the problem with magic was that it was impossible to resist. That was why it was called magic.

She could never act on her desire. The day had held a hint of poignancy, because it showed her everything that she'd never had. Everything that she'd never have.

So tonight she didn't just lie awake mulling over what she could do to keep her sisters together. Tonight, she lay awake because her blood fizzed with wanton curiosity and her skin ached for the brush of an elegant male hand. She'd thought the stranger was attractive when she met him, but as he recovered from his injuries, she'd found herself in physical thrall in a way that left her bewildered.

She'd always imagined that love was a spiritual emotion, involving hearts and souls. If this was love that she felt for her mysterious patient, it was astonishingly earthy. It was burning to touch and kiss and embrace. It was a painful, heavy, restless thrumming in the secret hollows of her body. It was lying sleepless in this bed, imagining all the forbidden things that Lancelot might do to her if she was a different woman. A free woman.

The pity of it all was that he might have commitments elsewhere. Did some other lucky woman claim the right to his kisses and caresses? To his smiles and conversation and company?

Anthea was a fool to be so besotted. She knew it. But knowing did nothing to calm the storm of yearning.

Nor did it help her to sleep, lying here and wishing against every law of morality that Lancelot shared this bed.

Perhaps she might settle down if she went downstairs and had a cup of chamomile tea. Might a book from the library distract her from sinful thoughts? Something stern and more suitable for Lent than Christmas.

Anthea sat up to light a candle, then slid out of bed. She put on her wrap and slippers – it was cold now that she'd forsaken the blankets – and let herself out into the dark corridor.

On her way to the steps, Anthea had to pass Lancelot's door. To her surprise, it was open. Even before she checked inside the room, she knew it would be empty. The bedclothes were as tumbled as hers, hinting that he'd also had trouble sleeping.

She heard Winifred's voice in her head, telling her to go back to bed. Telling her to lock her door.

No truly virtuous woman would go in search of a virile young man in the middle of the night. A truly virtuous woman would scuttle back to safety and say a grateful prayer that she'd discovered that he, too, roamed the house.

Anthea's heart had slammed to a stop when she realized that Lancelot shared her wakefulness. Now her pulses kicked into a wild gallop that made her head swim.

Excitement buzzing in her stomach, she continued along the corridor with a purposefulness that should make her cringe with shame. Her hand wasn't even trembling. The candle flame burned as steady as the beam from a lighthouse.

All she felt was expectation and curiosity. An odd charge in the air hinted that something momentous was about to happen, something to cherish through all the dreary years to come.

Anthea descended the staircase to the hall, where most of the Christmas greenery had ended up. The fresh scent of pine teased her nostrils.

She checked the library. It was empty. So was the rarely used dining room. Most of the time, she and the girls ate in the kitchen. The last room on this floor was the drawing room, where Lancelot had asked to kiss her yesterday afternoon.

When she'd denied him for fear of betraying her attraction to their audience. Edwina and Merry were too young to notice that Anthea couldn't play at kissing their guest. But Winifred watched her like a hawk, and Harriet was old enough to guess what was going on.

Anthea hovered in the doorway. Her gaze made a quick tour of the space. The fire glowed at the far end, but the room appeared to be empty.

Disappointment made her stagger. Lancelot wasn't here. Could he have gone down to the kitchen? He'd be warmer there. She was just about to turn away, not even pretending anymore that she wasn't looking for trouble, when a shadow moved in one of the big upholstered chairs in front of the fire.

Lancelot rose. He was dressed in his own clothes. "Anthea?"

Dear heaven, she'd gone looking for trouble, and she'd found it.

She stepped forward, her hand shaking so badly now that the candle sent flickering light dancing across the oak paneling. "You weren't in your room," she said in a low voice, then blushed at how much her remark revealed.

Did he think that she'd sneaked out of her bedroom in search of him? The awful truth was that she had, however much she might deny it. She braced for him to pick up on her admission, perhaps mock her. She couldn't bear any mockery. Not when she risked so much.

But he merely strode forward. "Here, give me that, before you drop it and burn the house down."

With a gentleness that made her asinine heart melt, he took the candle and set it on a small table near the door. He caught her hand and drew her into the room. Her shaking fingers curled around his, as if she feared falling. She did. Her knees wobbled, and she had trouble catching a complete breath.

Cold tinged the air, despite the fire. His touch was warm. Irresistibly so.

"Shall I close the door?" she murmured.

"Yes."

With reluctance, she released his hand and turned to shut the door. She knew it signaled her willingness to allow liberties. But he was a clever man. He must have known that from the moment she'd admitted that she sought him.

He took possession of her hand again. "Do we need mistletoe?"

The tender amusement in his voice reminded her how much she liked him. He'd made her smile so often, during these days when she'd been sure that all she'd think about was the family's departure from Yardley. Those touches of happiness were precious.

He was precious.

"No."

"You know I'm going to kiss you?"

What was the point of playing coy? "Yes."

"You wouldn't kiss me before."

"I was afraid that I might reveal..." With her free hand, she gestured to indicate everything that she was too shy to put into words.

"That you want me?"

"Yes."

"I want you."

"I...know."

"Of course you do. It's been hell keeping my hands off you."

It wasn't a surprise. She'd always known. But hearing him say the words aloud stirred a ripple of not-unpleasant trepidation. Her fingers tightened around his. "I don't mean..."

The fire's faint light revealed a smile of unusual sweetness on his lips. She was used to his ironic amusement, but now he looked as if she fulfilled all his dreams.

Be careful, Anthea. Don't turn this into anything more than a chance to find out what his kisses are like. Talking about dreams and forever only invites heartbreak.

"You've come for a few kisses," he said.

The tension eased from her shoulders. He understood. "That's risky enough."

"I swear you're safe."

She was sure that young men with mischief on their minds had made promises like that since the origins of humanity. Yet she believed him. She hoped to heaven that she wasn't mistaken.

"I trust you."

A troubled expression crossed his face. "Anthea, there's something we have to talk about first."

"No." She'd come so far, she couldn't brook any delay. "All we've done is talk. That's not why I'm here."

He frowned. "But..."

She lifted the hand she held and kissed his knuckles without breaking eye contact. "We'll talk later."

He exhaled on a long hiss and reached out to thread his fingers through the hair above her ear. "You're pure temptation."

"Then let me tempt you." She was in such a fever of anticipation, she hardly knew what she said. If he didn't kiss her in the next five minutes, she feared she'd explode.

His hand drifted down to the thick single braid confining her hair. He gave the long tail a gentle tug to bring her closer. She released his hand and with a tentative movement that belied her bold announcement, she placed her hand on his shoulder. He was warm, and she felt the strength of bone and sinew.

Since he'd arrived at Yardley, she'd touched him so often. It turned out that there was a universe of difference between caring for him as a patient and touching him now to invite his kiss.

"Kiss me, Anthea," he whispered and bent his head.

With a sigh, she lifted her face. Every cell of her body hungered for him. As she closed her eyes, time hung suspended for seconds that felt like an eon.

His mouth, like his voice, was soft as it brushed hers. The fleeting contact slammed through her like thunder. How could such a brief kiss shift the world off its axis? Yet it did.

She staggered as her knees turned to water, and her grip on his shoulder firmed to save her from falling. Or melting. Because that was what this felt like. Bones that had always been solid and reliable threatened to dissolve into honey.

A faint murmur of yearning escaped her. His lips descended, and this time he lingered. Torrents of heat rushed through her, and her mind began to whirl. She sagged and through the pounding in her blood, she felt him gather her up in his arms and bring her closer.

She'd known that he was tall and powerful since the day that she found him in the snow. But she'd never been so aware of his muscled potency as she was at this moment, with all that masculine hardness pressed up against her body.

Anthea gasped when the pressure of his lips deepened. His tongue slipped through for a brief taste of the interior of her mouth. The action was strange but stirring. It emphasized the intimacy blossoming between them.

He made a sound of approval and nipped at her lower lip. This time when his tongue entered her mouth, flames sizzled along her veins. That troubling, constant ache of need in the pit of her stomach expanded until she drowned in desire.

With a soft moan, she edged nearer to urge him on. For days, she'd imagined his kisses, but the reality of being in his arms flung her a thousand miles past even her most torrid daydreams.

His lips were hot, and he tasted like everything marvelous in the world. She wanted more. With shy eagerness, she fluttered her tongue against his. His growl was a wordless request to continue. Encouraged, she did it again.

The kiss had felt like fire from the moment that she'd allowed him to taste her mouth. Now it ignited into a raging blaze and sent her soaring to the stars.

The embrace transformed into a passionate dance. Anthea learned to copy what Lancelot did. Another nip on her lower lip. A sweep of his tongue along her upper lip. A breathtaking instant when he sucked her lower lip into his mouth. The glide of his tongue in her mouth, as though he savored her essence.

Her fantasies had proven so pallid compared to reality. Now they exploded to dust under the onslaught of a hundred variations in pleasure.

With her eyes closed, her other senses came alive. First, she basked in the radiant heat of his body and the way his arms enclosed her in a radiant circle. He smelled like heaven.

When she'd nursed him, they'd established a powerful physical intimacy. His spicy scent, tinged now with what she guessed was male arousal, lured her. She breathed in deep through the short interval when he abandoned her lips to kiss her face.

The sounds they made created the most stirring music. Soft, erratic breaths as he snatched air into his lungs between those astonishing kisses. Low purrs of approval that sounded like praise. The muttered release of her name, as he angled her face up for another breathtaking foray in their sensual journey.

Anthea discovered that she, too, was capable of a symphony of responses, however incoherent. Husky gasps of surprise and enjoyment. A faint moan of protest when he stopped kissing her to snatch a breath.

Kissing him, she began to explore the fascinating textures under her hands. The wide shoulders beneath the wool of his coat. He wasn't wearing a neckcloth, so his shirt gaped open across his chest. Her hands soon discovered the smooth skin of his throat then lowered to the soft whorls of hair on his pectorals. His body hair had intrigued her since she'd undressed him when he'd been out of his head with cold and exhaustion.

She raked one hand through the tangled curls on his head. Then lowered it to the back of his neck to bring him closer for more kisses. She wrapped her arms around him, testing the firm breadth of his back.

Lancelot conducted his own exploration, tracing her flanks and hips, running his hands down her arms. Her breasts swelled against his chest and the peaks hardened into aching points. Under her wrap and nightdress, she was naked. Now Lancelot knew that, too. Everywhere he touched, he made her burn for him.

He groaned against her lips and jutted his hips forward, until hard heat throbbed against her stomach. She should be alarmed, but his sexual demand stoked her excitement. She'd spent so long watching him and wanting him, this proof of desire was intoxicating.

She pressed shamelessly close, and her hands bunched in the superfine covering his back. The pulse between her legs accelerated until it shook her entire body.

He groaned again and ripped his lips free of hers. "Make me stop, Anthea."

"Stop," she whispered, burying her face in his throat and pressing a kiss to where his pulse raced above his collarbones.

"Sound like you mean it," he said, his voice rasping. His hands kneaded her hips with a rhythm that translated to the rush of her blood.

Instead, she snuggled closer. "I had no idea..."

"This is dangerous."

Still she clung to him. "Yes."

"And frustrating." She heard a hint of familiar wry humor. "I couldn't sleep before I came downstairs. I won't sleep a wink now."

"I couldn't stop thinking about you," she admitted. "I can't stop thinking about you."

"Anthea..." He sounded shaken.

This time, the descent into sensual paradise was immediate, like diving headfirst off a high cliff. She'd moved past self-consciousness. She just wanted him to keep on kissing her.

His lips left hers and before she could complain, he'd pushed her robe and nightdress away from her neck. When he kissed her there, her response was strong enough to make her cry out. Threads of fire spread a searing network of desire throughout her body.

This time, her knees really did give way and she only remained upright because his hands held her waist. When he scraped his teeth across a sensitive nerve, she saw fireworks. She fumbled for his arms and dug her fingers into his biceps.

She gave a shocked giggle. "That's depraved."

"It is."

He moved behind her to kiss the other side of her neck. Another jolt of sensation. Her chest heaving, she leaned back against him. She couldn't seem to drag in enough air to fill her lungs.

"I want to touch your breasts," he muttered, nibbling a sizzling line along her shoulder and ending with a sharp little bite at the top of her arm.

She jerked in his embrace. "You shouldn't."

"You still don't sound like you mean it."

"I don't," she said in despair. She'd reached such a pitch of craving that his request made her nipples tingle with longing. "But we can't..."

"I can control myself," he said, and she didn't bother pointing out that this time he sounded unconvinced.

Anthea tilted her head against his shoulder and nestled her rump into the cradle of his hips.

"Touch me," she murmured. She knew the risks that she took, but she was so lost in the unprecedented glory, she almost didn't care.

Feeling like lightning was about to strike, she waited to feel a man's hands on her breasts for the first time. When his palms brushed across her feminine flesh, she gasped and bumped backward.

He squeezed her gently and cupped her breasts in his hands in a way that made her core clench in carnal need. She closed her eyes. "Yes..."

Anthea glanced down to where he caressed her. Her robe hung loose, and her flannel nightgown tightened across her breasts to reveal beaded nipples. The sinful thought arose that he was a single layer of fabric away from touching her nakedness. But even mad for him as she was, she knew that if he undressed her, she'd end up surrendering too much.

When his hands covered her nipples, the heat inside her ignited to pure flame. He plucked at the crests, arrowing heat straight to her womb. The overwhelming liquid response had her pressing her thighs together in an attempt to find some relief from the gnawing hunger.

He began to kiss her nape. More sensation. More fevered response. Before tonight, she'd never guessed that a lover's touch could conjure pleasure from so many places on her body. As he nibbled along the edge of her hairline, she trembled and panted.

"I want to see you," he muttered, taking her earlobe between his teeth. Another unexpected surge of arousal.

"We can't," she responded on a wail.

"I know." He sounded as if he was in agony, too. One hand traced the slope of her breast and slid under the loose edge of her nightdress.

"Oh!" she squeaked as his hand met her skin. This time, when he toyed with her nipple, there was no barrier.

Anthea cried out again, rivers of heat blazing through her. She should stop him. She'd promised herself that she'd sample his kisses. Well, she'd done that. What she did now overstepped every boundary.

Lancelot's breath was a hoarse song in her ears. She was conscious of the jut of his rod against her rump. It would take very little to shatter his restraint.

The problem was that when everything he did was so miraculous, the idea of more was irresistible. Nevertheless, she must stop him. She must.

She must...

The slam of the door against the wall burst out of a different universe. Although the outraged voice was all too familiar.

"What in heaven's name is going on here? Anthea Bryars, get away from that scoundrel this instant!"

CHAPTER NINE

$\mathcal{A}$nthea wrenched free of Lancelot and stared aghast at Winifred, who regarded her with similar horror from the doorway. She wore a thick flannel nightdress, twin to the one Anthea had on, a white nightcap, and a plaid shawl. The candle that her old governess carried revealed every detail of her shock and dismay. And disappointment.

"Oh, hell..." he muttered, stepping between her and Winifred, as if he could stave off what was to come.

"Winifred!" Anthea gasped at the same time.

"Miss French, what an unexpected...surprise." Lancelot's composure returned faster than Anthea's. But then, she'd wager a hundred guineas she didn't have that he was more accustomed to being discovered in an illicit embrace than she was.

When Lancelot kissed Anthea and put his hands on her, she'd felt powerful and brave. Now under her friend's appalled gaze, she felt dirty and ashamed. With shaking hands, she dragged her robe around her and tied the belt, although she was mortifyingly aware that Winifred must have seen Lancelot toying with her breast.

"You owe Anthea your life. By what right do you put your filthy paws on her?"

"Don't speak to him like that, Winifred." Anthea had come back to herself enough to be angry as she shifted to stand beside Lancelot. "He didn't do anything that I didn't want him to do."

That didn't placate the woman. "That's no excuse. What on earth have you been up to, Annie? Don't tell me you've sneaked out every night to meet this villain."

Anthea's lips tightened. "He only left his sickbed this morning."

"You could have been creeping into his room."

"Anthea wouldn't do that, and you know it," Lancelot said.

"Once upon a time, I might have said that," Winifred retorted.

"She has nothing to apologize for."

While Anthea appreciated his ongoing defense, they both knew that it wasn't true. Even worse, they both knew how close they'd come to abandoning good intentions and taking their caresses past the point of no return.

"You were...fondling her bosom," Winifred said in disgust. "I know what I saw."

"That's enough, Miss French," Lancelot said with an autocratic edge that startled Anthea. Goodness, he sounded like the lord of the manor.

"I speak as I see." The imperious manner had no power over Winifred. "And what I see does neither you nor Anthea any credit."

Beside her, Anthea felt him bristle. "Save your scolding for the person who deserves it, and that's not Anthea. If anyone is to blame here, it's me."

"I have no doubt," Winifred said.

"I'm a grown woman and if I want to kiss a man, I can." Despite what she said, Anthea felt sick with guilt and humiliation. "I'm twenty-five years old, not fifteen."

Winifred's lips flattened. "And I suppose if you want to go to the devil, you can do that, too."

For heaven's sake, this threatened to become an all-out row. That would do nobody any good and might wake her sisters. While Anthea was ready to stand up for herself in front of Winifred, she'd hate Harriet or Merry or Edwina to know what she'd been doing.

"I suppose I can," Anthea hissed in a low voice, still trying to brave it out, although her cheeks felt hot enough to catch fire. "You have no real authority over me."

Winifred didn't back down, although Anthea caught a flash of hurt in her expression. "No, perhaps I don't, since you've taken that independence in your own two hands and given away all your common sense in return. However, I'll remind you that three young girls in this house worship the ground you walk on. What sort of example does this set for them?"

What remained of Anthea's shaky defiance shattered. She'd spent most of her life caring for her sisters. She'd been selfish to think that she could steal a moment of joy without counting how any fall from grace would affect Harriet, Merry, and Edwina. "This doesn't concern the girls."

"Don't be more of a ninnyhammer than you are already," Winifred snapped. "How can it not concern the girls?"

"If you're angry at anyone, be angry at me." Lancelot reached for Anthea's hand, but she shifted out of reach.

"Oh, I'm angry at you, all right," Winifred said.

Anthea should be grateful that her friend had turned up to save her from doing something irrevocable. She wasn't quite there yet, but now that the sensual madness receded, her conscience was shrieking at her like a thousand enraged devils.

"All we did was kiss each other," Anthea said, wringing her hands and wishing she could disappear into a hole in the ground. "I'm not a fallen woman."

Although she was uncomfortably aware that after a few more kisses, her claims to virtue would be moot.

"So you say."

"Anthea has a right to a private life," Lancelot said, still trying to defend her, bless him.

Anyway he was wrong. She didn't. Not really. Not when she was responsible for three young lives.

"And I have a right to my opinion." Winifred glowered at him, then turned her attention to Anthea. "I also have a right to tell someone I've always loved when she's acting like a fool. Annie, you know nothing about this man."

"I know enough to like him."

"Hmph."

She injected a conciliatory note into her voice. "There's nothing to be gained by quarreling. I'm going back to bed, and I think you should, too."

Winifred cast Anthea and Lancelot a narrow-eyed glare. "Can I trust you both to stay in your rooms?"

Anthea's temper, already shaky with mortification and the anguish of being ripped from heaven to hell without a moment's warning, flared. "I'm leaving before I say something I'll regret."

"Before you *do* something you'll regret, rather," Winifred replied in an acid tone.

"Anthea's right. It's time this discussion ended." Lancelot extended his arm to her. "May I escort you upstairs?"

Winifred's eyes narrowed on Anthea as she answered. "No, thank you."

He stepped back and bowed with more of that lordliness. When she'd first found him, she'd noted his natural arrogance. She'd forgotten that until now. "As you wish."

Winifred glanced between them and nodded, apparently satisfied that neither of them plotted further misbehavior. "I'll walk up with you."

"I don't want your company right now, thank you." As both passion and anger ebbed, leaving only embarrassment and self-loathing behind, Anthea felt like a trampled flower. She was desperate for some privacy.

"Very well." Winifred turned away and stepped out into the hall.

"Anthea, can you wait a minute?" Lancelot said under his breath, reaching for her arm. "I'm so sorry this happened, my dear."

Despite everything, his touch sent a blast of heat through her and provided an unwelcome reminder of how close she'd verged to forgetting everything but desire. The awful truth was that she feared she'd do it all again, given the chance.

She shook off his hold. "It's too late to be sorry."

"I have something important to say. Please. I won't take long."

She wasn't sure that she could endure hearing him disavow their kisses. Nonetheless she hesitated, before she noticed Winifred glaring back at her from halfway across the hall. "Anything you need to say can wait for daylight."

The angle of his jaw expressed displeasure, but he bowed and stepped back. "Give me half an hour after breakfast, then."

"Very well."

She avoided his eyes, as queasy remorse soured her stomach. The reality of what had happened here was sinking in and becoming more and more unbearable. No wonder Winifred was livid. How could Anthea have let things progress to a point where she was about to give herself to him? For the love of God, she didn't even know his name, let alone whether he was married.

"Anthea?" Winifred said.

"I'm coming, Winifred," she mumbled.

Picking up her candle with a shaking hand, she left the drawing room. Lancelot's gaze burned into her back with every step she took away from him.

Christopher woke to the sound of his door crashing open. He cracked scratchy eyes, hoping to see Anthea. Instead, to his regret, it was Miss French. Given that he'd stayed awake for hours after coming upstairs, berating himself for taking things so far with Anthea, he didn't feel like he needed another lecture.

Although if he was honest, he'd also devoted too much time to recalling how delicious Anthea's kisses had been. He'd spent hours trapped in his sickbed, imagining the taste of those voluptuous pink lips. Yet the glorious reality eclipsed his fantasies the way the sun outshone the moon.

Last night, he'd cursed Winifred to Hades when she barged in. Now he admitted they were lucky that she had. He'd had no intentions of ruining Anthea, but passion had exploded so fast that he'd come close to forgetting his honor.

"Don't pretend you're not awake," she said in a hectoring tone.

He groaned and rolled away. "You don't need to say anything. I'm well aware I did the wrong thing. I should have sent Anthea back to bed the moment she arrived."

"Yes, you should." She shut the door behind her. "Your behavior was disgraceful."

It had been. He'd kissed Anthea under false pretenses. While he'd tried to tell her who he was – twice – he hadn't pushed as hard as he might to confess all.

Guilt churning in his belly, Christopher pushed upright against the pillows. He was back in the deuced nightshirt, although right now he was glad that he hadn't gone to bed naked as he did in London.

"Don't be angry with Anthea. We met by accident, not by design. That's the one and only time we've been together like that." He wasn't used to apologizing for his misdeeds, but he couldn't bear Winifred to chide Anthea for what wasn't her fault. "You have my word that kisses were all that took place."

"Kisses were enough."

To his regret, Winifred was right. "Believe me, you can't despise me half as much as I despise myself."

"I wouldn't say that." With an audible thunk, Winifred set the jug of hot water she carried onto the floor. "You're deceiving that girl. We both know you are. You've been lying from the day you arrived."

His guilt sharpened to the point of nausea. "Lying?"

She stepped up to stand at the base of the bed. Her lined face was stern. "If you don't tell her who you are today, my lord, I will."

The ground dropped out from beneath Christopher. Or at least that was how it felt.

He gaped at Winifred. The "my lord" revealed that as far as Winifred was concerned, his disguise was no disguise at all. "I was injured when I came here."

"Yes, you were." Winifred looked if possible even more disgusted. "But there's nothing wrong with your memory. There never has been, has there, Lord Denton?"

It was almost a relief to have his identity out in the open, however correct his predictions proved that his unmasking would result in the residents of Yardley Hall despising him. He realized now that Winifred had never accepted his claims of amnesia. She'd always reacted halfheartedly to his pretense.

"How did you know?"

Winifred folded her arms in front of her substantial bosom. "At least you're not denying it."

"I tried to tell her."

"Not too hard, I'd say, given it's a matter of three words."

Christopher didn't know what the devil was the matter with him, but he could only think of one relevant set of three words. He couldn't see that saying "I love you" was going to sort out this tangle. "Three words?"

Winifred looked unimpressed. "'I'm Lord Denton.' Although, you could go on to say that you're responsible for throwing these poor mites out into the snow at Christmas, but Anthea already knows that."

He hid a wince, however deserving the criticism. "Everyone else believed me, including that quack of a doctor."

Christopher waited for her to defend Hobson, but she didn't. Instead, that shrewd gaze remained leveled on his face.

She must be a hell of a governess. Her charges wouldn't get away with a thing. Even he, rich, sophisticated, careless of conventional morality, shifted uncomfortably under that gimlet regard.

"How did I give myself away?" he asked.

"Yes, well, I'm too old and jaded for you to bamboozle me with charm and good looks. Not to mention, I've seen a fair bit more of the world than Anthea and her sisters. Anyway, who else would be riding to Yardley through a blizzard in a suit of London clothes that cost more than every dress folded up in my armoire? Who on earth else can you be, if you aren't the new owner on his way to see his inheritance?"

"I've been a villain," he said in a low voice. "I should have told you everything when I regained my senses."

"Yes, you should. Your ruse wasn't even convincing. If you genuinely didn't know who you were, you'd be beside yourself with worry. You took it all like a stroll in Hyde Park."

She had a point. "So why haven't you told Anthea?"

"I wanted to wait and see what your game is." She paused. "Also I hoped once you realized the damage you'd done, you might have a change of heart about throwing us out."

"The eviction was all a terrible mistake. When I inherited, I had no idea my cousins existed. If I'd known, I'd never have asked them to leave."

"So why haven't you said anything by now?"

Christopher sighed, feeling despicable and not much liking it. "It's no great mystery. Everyone loathes Wicked Cousin Christopher, and everyone seems to have a soft spot for Lancelot."

"You're just putting off the evil moment. You have to admit your identity at some stage."

He ran his hand through his hair. "I know."

"And kissing Anthea last night without telling her who you are was a heinous thing to do."

Self-disgust twisted his gut. "Yes, it was. Which is why I've asked her to grant me an interview after breakfast so I can confess. You haven't said anything that my conscience hasn't already pointed out."

"It's a relief to hear that you've got a conscience." Winifred showed no sign of softening. "Seeing that you claim to harbor a principle or two, I hope you intend to do something to secure a future for your cousins."

"I do indeed." *And Anthea. And even you, you interfering old biddy.* Although despite his discomfort, he couldn't help commending Winifred's courage in bearding him in his den.

"That's enough to be going on with, then," she said, turning to go.

He spoke as she reached the door. "Will Anthea hate me?"

"I don't know." Winifred glanced back with a somber expression. "I do know that she's a woman with no tolerance for dishonesty, and you've lied to her from the beginning."

On that unencouraging note, Winifred left him alone with his confusion and his guilt and his desperate longing.

Impatient with deceit and his own games and his fear of losing Anthea's good opinion, Christopher had a quick shave. Then he dressed in a careless hurry that would have shocked his starchy valet.

He rushed downstairs to the hall to find Anthea standing at a table at the base of the stairs. She was rearranging a chaotic vase of holly that Edwina had put together yesterday.

As he appeared around the turn in the staircase, she glanced up. He'd wondered whether she might feel awkward or shy this morning, especially given how their embrace had ended. But her lips curled up in a radiant smile that set his heart cartwheeling.

She set down the vase and stepped toward him. "Good morning."

He took the last few steps two at a time and somehow found himself holding her hand, once he reached the floor. "Good morning. Did you sleep?"

"Not much. What about you?"

"Hardly a wink. Kisses will do that to you."

"I wouldn't know."

"You do now."

She made a perfunctory attempt to pull free. "Someone might come."

"Let them. We're under the mistletoe."

Her short laugh vibrated with excitement. "We're not, you know."

"Then let's find some." He looked around and noticed a bunch suspended from a dark and rather oppressive seascape near the fireplace.

"Don't you want to talk to me?"

"I always want to talk to you."

That made her laugh again. "But you'd rather kiss me."

"My oath, yes." But instead of sweeping her across to the mistletoe, the man of honor who lurked mostly unacknowledged in his soul howled in protest.

He had no right to woo this exceptional girl until she knew who he was. Apprehension settled cold and heavy in his gut. Once Anthea knew the truth, would she ever smile at him again? He knew without any doubt that a world that didn't include Anthea's smiles wasn't worth living in.

"I'm pleased to hear that."

Christopher steeled himself for what he must do, even as he basked in the glow in her blue eyes. Once he told her, would she still look at him as if he was the Christmas present that she'd always wanted? By God, he prayed she would.

"First, we really must talk. I can't wait until after breakfast."

He read surprise and curiosity in her expression. It was clear that she expected something nice. He could hardly bear to spoil her day, but Miss French was right. It was unconscionable to pursue Anthea when she didn't know who he was.

"That sounds intriguing."

"I hope you'll think so." She could have no idea how sincere he was about that. He kept hold of her hand. "Let's go into the library. I don't want to be interrupted."

"Lancelot..." A blush brightened her creamy cheek.

One benefit of telling her the truth was that nobody would ever call him bloody Lancelot again. As he began to draw her across to the corridor, a loud knock came at the front door.

Both of them stopped in shock. Apart from Dr. Hobson, nobody had visited the house in all the time that Christopher had been here. The inclement weather had kept Yardley Hall as isolated as Robinson Crusoe's island.

"Who can that be?" Anthea asked.

Another knock.

"Let somebody else find out," Christopher said urgently. "I've got something important to say."

"But this might be important, too. If it wasn't, whoever it is would stay by their own fireside, with it so cold out."

"Harriet or Winifred can look after them."

Another knock with a hint of impatience.

Harriet appeared from the corridor. "Who on earth is that?"

"I don't know," Anthea muttered, snatching her hand free of Christopher's, as her sister's interested stare took in the interaction.

"Why don't you let them in and find out?"

Anthea was blushing like fire now. "Why don't you?"

Harriet bustled over to lift the heavy latch and open the door. Frosty air blasted into the hall. "Mr. Parsons, good morning."

"Aye, good morning to you, Miss Harriet. Sorry for intruding, but I've been waiting for a break in the weather so I could get up to the hall."

Christopher stood next to Anthea and observed a middle-aged man wrapped in a thick sheepskin coat and clutching a battered hat in one hand.

"He's one of the tenants," Anthea murmured before she stepped forward. "Good morning, Mr. Parsons. Is there some problem? I hope nobody in the family is ill."

"Aye, all well, Miss Anthea. God be thanked. The young uns are all agog for Christmas tomorrow."

Harriet stepped back to allow the man to come in off the front step. "So how can we help?"

"I think more rightly I'm about to help you." He edged inside, and Harriet closed the door after him. "Or at least the new lord of the manor, like."

"Lord..." Anthea said in a fading voice.

"Aye." Parsons fastened his attention on Christopher and bowed. "I'm guessing you're Lord Denton, sir? If so, my boy Jem has your horse outside."

Through the thunder of his heart, Christopher was aware of Anthea stiffening at his side. For dread of what his face might reveal, he didn't dare look at her.

He strode forward. "Parsons, is it?"

"Aye, my lord." The man twisted his hat in his hands. "I rent Primrose Farm over the other side of the hill."

"Thank you for keeping Mistral safe. I had no idea what became of him. I fell off on my way here, and the beast bolted. I was worried he was halfway to Ludlow by now."

He felt Harriet staring at him. When he cast her a quick glance, he wished he hadn't. She looked utterly horrified. He chanced a peek at Anthea. She was as white as the snow outside. Avoiding his eyes, she reached out to grab the stair rail. She looked as if someone had just dealt her a body blow, damn it.

"Lucky you found your way to the hall, then, sir." Parsons gave his audience a curious glance, as if sensing something amiss.

"Yes, it was. And lucky Mistral found his way to you, too." Christopher wished Harriet or Anthea would say something. Their thorny silence made him feel queasy. "This is no weather to be wandering around about in, for man or beast."

"A few days ago, we caught young Dr. Hobson on his way to the hall. He told us there was a man up at the manor who'd had an accident in the woods. When not long after, a fine black gelding ambled into the barn as gentle as a lamb, we knew the man at the manor had to be the owner. Nobody else comes to

Yardley, particular in the middle of a blizzard. When no one came to collect the horse, we opened the saddlebags. I hope you don't mind, but we knew anyone who'd lost bloodstock like him would want him back. We saw papers with Lord Denton's name, so that's when we guessed who he belonged to."

"I don't mind at all."

With a slight frown, Parsons bobbed his head again. "Should I get Jem to put...Mistral in the stables, Miss Anthea?" Then he realized that perhaps Anthea was no longer in authority. "My lord? My lad often works with the hall's livestock. He do know his way about, and it would save you all coming out into the cold."

"Thank you, but I might step out with you and take a look at Mistral." Still Anthea didn't speak, although Christopher could feel her eyes boring into his back. "Once the weather clears, I'll call by the farm and talk to you about compensation."

Parsons dipped his head. "No need for that, sir. We all help each other in the valley."

"Nonetheless, I'm very grateful, and I'll see you right."

"Thank 'ee, my lord."

"Now, your boy will be getting cold out there and I'm sure you want to get off back to your fireside, seeing it's Christmas Eve. I'll take over from here."

"Aye, sir, it do be a good day for getting cozy at home."

Glancing at neither Anthea nor Harriet, Christopher trudged toward the door. His heart felt like a stone in his chest.

Parsons paused on his way out and cast another uncertain look behind him. "Wishing you both a happy Christmas, Miss Anthea and Miss Harriet."

After a bristling silence, Harriet responded in an unnaturally high voice. "Thank you, Mr. Parsons. Best wishes to you and the family."

Christopher followed the man down into the snow, where a boy of about fourteen held Mistral's bridle. Both horse and lad looked pleased to see him.

"Hello, old son," Christopher said, as the horse stretched his neck out in welcome. "I was sure you and I were parted forever."

The horse nickered and his ears flicked, as his master patted his neck and checked him for injury. To Christopher's relief, Mistral was in fine fettle. "Thank you, Jem and Mr. Parsons. You've taken excellent care of him. I won't forget it."

"Aye, he's a good horse. Best I've ever seen. Nice you spending Christmas with your kin, too. We're all terrible fond of the ladies at the manor here on the Yardley estate, my lord. Talk is that they're leaving. That would be a crying shame."

Despite everything, Christopher couldn't help smiling to hear the man defend Anthea and her sisters. "We're working something out. My cousins won't suffer because I've taken over the estate, Mr. Parsons. You have my word on it."

"That's good to hear. I'll be off then. A merry Christmas to you, my lord."

"And to you and your family, Parsons."

Jem passed across the reins and walked away through the snow at his father's side. Christopher took a brief scan of the sky, which promised more snow to come. Although he doubted it was going to be anywhere near as icy as the reception that he was about to receive inside the house.

"Lord Denton?" Harriet had put on a coat and was coming down the stairs.

He looked up, not sure what to expect. "Yes?"

"I'll look after your horse. I think you need to talk to Anthea."

"Thank you." He handed her the reins. "I'm sorry that I turned out to be Wicked Cousin Christopher."

"So am I." The wary expression in her clear gray eyes saddened him. "Although it's up to you quite how wicked you intend to be."

"Thank you for giving me a chance."

She shrugged. "I liked Lancelot. Perhaps a little bit of him still lives inside you."

"Quite a lot, I should think. Is Anthea waiting in the hall?"

"No, she's gone into the library."

"Bless you, Harry." Desperate to make things right with Anthea, he raced up the steps and through the open door.

CHAPTER TEN

When Christopher opened the library door, Anthea was standing looking out the window. He noticed how fast her shoulders straightened, but not fast enough for him to miss their posture of uncharacteristic defeat.

His gut, already weighted with guilt and self-hatred, tightened painfully. By God, he should have announced who he was that first night. The next morning at the very latest. And borne the brunt of being the man everyone hated.

Although even now, he couldn't regret getting to know Anthea over these last few days. The sweetness of her company – for heaven's sake, the joy of kissing her – was unprecedented in his self-indulgent life.

What a rotten sod he was. Talk about trying to have his cake and eat it, too. He wanted Anthea to like him and desire him and seek him out. Even now, he was trying to wriggle out of the consequences of his deception, despite knowing that he'd dealt this lovely girl a shattering blow.

She was right to despise him, as he feared she must.

"Go away." She didn't turn around, and the thickness in her voice told him that she was crying.

Sick with remorse, he closed the door. "Anthea..."

"But I have no power to tell you to go away, do I? Because you have every right to be here and I don't."

Her bitter tone sliced like razors. "Darling, don't."

The endearment made her whirl to face him. He saw tears on her face. "Don't you call me that."

He spread his hands. "But you are my darling."

If he'd expected that to appease her, he was to be disappointed. Her cheeks might be wet, but her eyes glittered with fury. She surveyed him as if he was a cockroach crawling across the carpet. "I'm not your darling. I'm your dupe."

The breath jammed in his throat. By all that was holy, she was superb. Like a queen. He'd admired her from the first, almost as much as he'd wanted her. Seeing her now, incandescent with righteous rage, he realized that there wasn't a woman in the world to match her.

He didn't just admire and want her. He loved her. With every ounce of his black heart.

And because he'd lied, he had a grim feeling that he'd lost any chance to win her. "It wasn't all falsehood."

"Yes, it was. Because everything you said, everything you did was based on deceit."

"I'm sorry, Anthea. So sorry. I know an apology is inadequate recompense for my wrongs against you, but it's all I have. I should have told you everything long before this."

"Yes, you should." She swallowed and clenched her hands at her sides. Fury made her voice shake. "How dare you encourage my confidences? How dare you make us all care for you? How dare you pretend you were fond of us? How dare you...*kiss* me last night and act like that meant anything to you, other than a joke? How dare you, my lord?"

Every word felt like a stone pitched his head. Most bruising of all was the "my lord" at the end, bitten off like a deadly insult.

"My name is Christopher," he said. *Wicked Cousin Christopher.*

A savage swipe of her hand swept his words away. She sucked in a shuddering breath. "What the devil do I care? I hope you had a good laugh at how you weaseled your way into our affections. For pity's sake, if Winifred hadn't come in last night, heaven knows what might have happened. You would have had great entertainment to keep you laughing all the way back to London."

"Anthea, I'm not laughing," he said in a choked voice. He loathed that he'd hurt her, but everything he did just made things worse. "You're breaking my heart."

Outrage flared in her eyes. "You don't have a heart."

He did, and it belonged to her. Forever. But it would do him no good to say that now. Perhaps ever. At this instant, she hated him. Worse, she despised him. The sodding pity of it all was that he deserved it.

"You make everything sound much more calculated than it was," he said, knowing that was no excuse.

Her eyes sharpened. "Was there ever a stage when you didn't remember your name?"

For a charged second, he wondered if he could claim that he really had lost his memory, at least at first. Then his shoulders slumped in despair. Hadn't his lies already done enough harm?

"No, I always knew who I was," he said, desolation weighting his answer.

"I thought so." He watched another level of misery crash down upon her, although she expressed no surprise. "How you must have chuckled to watch us all run around serving you and falling under your spell, when you knew from the first that you were going to throw us out to fend for ourselves. What a grand tale that will make for your London cronies."

"Stop bloody saying that," he snapped. "Nobody's laughing."

"Just tell me one thing. Do you still intend to abandon your cousins to poverty?"

At least that was one issue he could settle. "No. You and your sisters have a home at Yardley for as long as you want one."

She sagged like a marionette with cut strings. "That's something, I suppose."

He took no comfort from her words. She still sounded like she couldn't abide him. "Whatever you think of me, the girls are safe."

She raised a shaking hand to dash the moisture from her cheeks. "Why didn't you tell us the truth when you arrived? It seems so cruel. I don't understand."

He sighed, feeling like the lowest worm in creation. "I'm not lying when I say I don't remember much about that first night, but I remember everything else. I'd taken about a week to ride from London to Shropshire, although it was madness to stay on the road when the weather closed in. I didn't want to go to my mother for Christmas, so I thought I'd come up and have a look at Uncle Basil's manor house. I assumed the place would be empty."

"Because you'd given us notice without a thought for what became of us," she said sourly.

By all that was holy, he wished he could claim some honorable action in all this. But he'd done the wrong thing from the outset. "I didn't know you or the girls existed. Uncle Basil never said a word about you. The solicitor just mentioned there were tenants and that he'd given them notice in preparation for me taking possession."

"You could have found out."

"I'm bloody sorry I didn't. I know how tough it's been for you since Basil died and left your future up in the air."

Her lips tightened. "Yes, because I told you. Because I was stupid enough to think you and I had become friends."

He forked his hand through his hair, as he cursed himself yet again. "You weren't stupid. You aren't. I was very happy to be your friend."

More than that, if she'd let him, but that was before she'd decided that she hated him. How the hell could he endure it?

"Friends don't lie to each other," she said flatly, retreating a pace.

What could he say to that? He plunged on with his stumbling explanation, already knowing it wouldn't restore him to favor. "Then when I woke up in the blue room the next morning and I had my wits about me, Edwina was performing a horrid little puppet show where she beat Christopher Trant to death. It still gives me shivers."

"Those dolls. She's quite savage, isn't she?"

"Terrifying," he said with a theatrical shudder.

Usually that would amuse Anthea, but not today. "I should have stopped her, I suppose. But ever since she heard that we had to leave Yardley, she's been afraid and angry. It's hard enough for the others, but at least they're old enough to understand that sometimes necessity can be harsh. Edwina's just a baby. I hoped killing Cousin Christopher helped her to deal with her fears."

"It didn't do much for actual Cousin Christopher."

"I'm sure." Her tone held no sympathy.

He reached a point where he'd give her half his fortune, if she'd grant him a kind word. Her coldness was a painful reminder of how he'd basked in the warmth of her regard since they'd met. He knew that he'd earned her dislike, but he felt as if she locked him out into the snow to freeze. Kill Cousin Christopher indeed.

Knowing nothing he said could make up for what he'd done, he forced himself to continue. "At that stage, I was puzzled and rather wary, so I decided to play for time and discover what was going on."

"That can't have taken you long. All of us decided you were the perfect confidant."

Another stab of excruciating guilt. Because he had exerted himself to beguile. He was well aware that he hadn't just betrayed Anthea. He'd betrayed her sisters as well. "Not Winifred."

"No, Winifred never took to you, did she?" Anthea said, as if she found the answer to a puzzling riddle.

"She'd guessed who I was, you see. Although I only found that out today."

Anthea looked annoyed. "Why didn't she tell me?"

"She said she wanted to see what I was up to. After what happened last night, she decided she couldn't delay my unmasking any longer. This morning, she told me that unless I revealed my identity, she would."

Anthea winced. "That's what you wanted to talk to me about."

"Yes." They were both aware that it was too little too late.

"And you tried to tell me last night, too."

"Yes, but I couldn't resist kissing you instead."

Her lips turned down, and color tinged her cheeks. At least she'd stopped crying, but he took no hope from that. Her manner grew frostier with every second. A fire might burn in the hearth, but he didn't feel its effects under the arctic blast of her blue eyes.

"You must have been so bored, stuck in a bedroom with a gaggle of rustics to entertain you. I'm guessing your life in London is crammed with glamour and spectacle and debauchery."

The disdain in her voice made him flinch. "What do you want me to say?"

"The truth." She shot him a furious glare. "However difficult that might be for you."

Christopher remained a million miles away from mercy. He knew it, but every reminder stung. "Yes, up until now, I've taken advantage of the diversions available to a rich man with no commitments. I have no reason to apologize for that. But you're wrong about one thing. I didn't kiss you because I was bored."

Shame dimmed her gaze, and he realized that however much she chastised him, she was even harder on herself. "I suppose my penchant for you made me so ridiculous, that you kissed me out of pity."

Despite everything, that provoked a brief laugh. "Don't be a ninny, Anthea. You might be innocent, but you're not *that* innocent." He took no comfort from hearing that she had a weakness for him. That clearly didn't make up for the revelation of his identity. "We both know I kissed you because I was mad for you. Seeing you every day and not being able to take you into my arms was driving me out of my mind."

His admission didn't mollify her either. "Was that why you lied, because you knew I'd never kiss the man who was splitting up my family?"

He sighed. "I can't claim anything like that much guile."

"I wouldn't know," she said with an edge that cut. "I don't know anything about you."

"Of course you do. At first, curiosity kept me quiet. Then I discovered I liked you all so much, I couldn't bear to tell you that I was Cousin Christopher. Everyone seemed fond of Lancelot. Everyone hated Christopher."

"Lancelot doesn't exist. He never did." She narrowed her eyes on him. "Are you married?"

Appalled, he gaped at her. "For pity's sake, Anthea, no, I'm not married. I have a few scruples."

She didn't soften. "Not as far as I can see. Are you promised to anyone?"

Yes, to you, my love. "No. I'm entirely eligible."

"Only in the most worldly terms. If we take character into consideration, you have nothing to offer."

The bleak certainty in her words made him want to smash something. "Have I ruined everything between us forever?" he asked in a stark tone.

She regarded him as if he was a stranger. Of all the many injuries he'd suffered today, that hurt the most. This was why he hadn't told her who he was. But now she knew, and they were estranged anyway.

"There can be nothing between us, when it's all based on lies."

Aghast, he stared at her. At last, he admitted that he'd hoped, in spite of everything he'd done, that he could talk her around, charm his way back into her good graces.

But he'd underestimated her. She was a woman of strength and integrity, and she'd never forgive him.

Everything was lost. There was no point trying to convince her to accept his apology.

"I'm sorry, Anthea. You have no idea how sorry. If I could do it all again differently, I would, but it's too late for that." Feeling like he'd swallowed corrosive acid, he straightened and stepped back with a deep bow. There was nothing to keep him at Yardley, apart from the memories of the happiest days he could remember. "I'll leave straightaway. Mistral looks to be in good shape. He'll get me to Shrewsbury. I won't bother you anymore."

She glanced out the window where a curtain of snow turned everything white. "You can't go in this. I didn't save your life a few days ago for you to throw it away on Christmas Eve."

In genuine dismay, he took note of the weather. "But you'd like me to go."

Anthea didn't answer that. She didn't have to.

"It's your house. We're the trespassers." She made a hopeless gesture. "We should be the ones to go."

Another bleak grunt of laughter escaped. "I know my name in this house is mud, but even that villain Cousin Christopher wouldn't turn three young girls, an old lady, and a damsel in distress out into a blizzard."

Her shoulders tightened, and she glared at him. "I'm no damsel in distress."

"No," he said softly and sadly. "You're magnificent."

For a long interval, she surveyed him, and he watched her proud shell crack. She might pretend to be made of ice, but beneath her façade of control, she was a seething mess of misery and guilt and anger.

With him and with herself. Because in spite of all he'd done, he was sure that she hadn't stopped wanting him. He knew to his cost that wishing alone couldn't banish desire and affinity and longing.

He'd flinched under her rage, but this was worse. This showed him how his cowardice had wounded her. Because the unwelcome truth was that he had tried to attract her interest. And he'd succeeded. She'd never have kissed him, unless she felt the same delight in him as he felt in her.

Christopher took an unsteady pace forward, wondering if despite everything, she might spare a speck of forgiveness to soothe the anguish in his soul.

When she stiffened in immediate rejection, he stopped where he stood. He didn't deserve her forgiveness. Perhaps before last night, he could have justified his sins. The moment he'd kissed her as Lancelot instead of Lord Denton, he'd shattered any possibility of trust.

"You'll be with us for Christmas," she said in a voice like broken glass. "I hope you'll do your best to pretend that you're not too unhappy about that. I'd like the day to be special for the girls."

Good Lord, he'd been so desperate to make his peace with Anthea that he'd forgotten that he needed to make reparations to his cousins as well. "Harriet will have told Merry and Edwina by now."

"I imagine so."

"I'd better go and make my apologies."

"Yes."

"Will you please try and pardon me?" he asked, knowing he wasted his time.

"What can my forgiveness matter to the great Lord Denton?" she asked, her tone like a whip. "I wish you good day, my lord."

She dipped into a deep curtsy. The gesture of respect toward his title conveyed nothing but endless contempt.

CHAPTER ELEVEN

Christopher found his cousins and Winifred in the kitchen. On such an icy day, it was the warmest room in the house. It must be mere fancy to be convinced that he'd never feel warm again.

When he appeared in the doorway, silence crashed down. Of course they were talking about him.

Four faces turned toward him, showing a range of reactions. From where she stirred a pot over the stove, Winifred sent him a glare of weary disdain. Nothing new there. Harriet leaped up from the table and regarded him with a sympathetic expression. He suspected that he must appear rather battered after his encounter with Anthea. Merry looked wary, as she rose from her chair more slowly. Wary, but not hostile. Edwina was perched on a stool near the fire with Jenny on her lap. She scowled at him, as if she wished her dolls had murdered him in fact rather than in play.

Before he could speak, Merry stepped forward. "So you're really Wicked Cousin Christopher?"

"I am." He spread his hands in apology. "I'm sorry."

"So are we," said Harriet. "We were very fond of Lancelot."

He took a pace forward. "I hope when you get to know me, you might summon up some affection for Christopher, too. I promise you he's not half so odious as you imagine. And he's very fond of all of you. It would be a pity if you decided you couldn't stand him."

Merry frowned. "You're not going to throw us out into the snow?"

He mustered a smile. "If I throw you out, I'll have nobody to kiss under the mistletoe. Which would be a pity when it took me a devil of an age to put it all up."

To his relief, Merry looked less on edge, but Harriet sent him a searching look. "What about after Christmas?"

"I'll need help to take down all that greenery. Not to mention, if everyone deserts me, who will be here to celebrate New Year's Eve?"

"So when do we have to go?" Merry asked, serious as ever.

"You don't have to go at all."

Winifred exhaled with audible relief and for once, the glance she bestowed upon him was almost approving. Harriet frowned, as if she wasn't quite sure that she understood. "Ever?"

"Not unless you want to."

"But what about the letter from your solicitor?" Merry asked.

"That dunderhead is no longer my solicitor, and as the owner of Yardley Hall, I decide who lives here. I'm hoping it will be my newfound cousins."

Harriet looked bewildered. "But why..."

He sighed and tunneled his hand through his hair. "Until I arrived, I had no idea that I had such delightful relations waiting in Shropshire. Uncle Basil never mentioned you. Nor did his lawyer. I was appalled when I discovered what that idiot had done, telling you to get out like that. I'm just so grateful that I found my way here while you were in residence, so I had a chance to remedy my mistake."

"So no Great-Aunt Dorcas?" Harriet asked with a tentative hope that made him feel even guiltier than he already did.

"No Great-Aunt Dorcas."

"And no Quillan Seminary and Missionary Society for Distressed Gentlewomen?" Merry asked.

That provoked a startled laugh. "Good Lord, is that the name of the school? It sounds dire."

"We were dreading it," Merry said.

"I can imagine."

"So we can all stay together?"

"Yes, indeed, you can."

Merry and Harriet shared a glance. "In that case, we'll have to stop calling you Wicked Cousin Christopher," Harriet said with a tremulous smile that made him feel, for the first time in ages, that he might have done something right.

"I would hope so. Christopher is perfectly fine."

"But you're Lord Denton," Merry said, regarding him with doubt in her eyes.

"You're my family. Family don't need to stand on ceremony. Now you know we're cousins, perhaps you can give me a Christmas hug to tell me I'm forgiven." He studied the three girls. "That is if I *am* forgiven?"

As he'd expected, Harriet was the first to move in his direction. She rose on her tiptoes to press a kiss to his cheek. "I'm ready to forgive you, Nice

Cousin Christopher, especially if it means we keep our home."

An unfamiliar lump of emotion blocked his throat. Despite the hellish mess with Anthea, he could never be sorry that he'd found these marvelous additions to his family. "Always, Harry."

Merry was next. She gave him a quick peck on the cheek then danced out of reach. "I'm happy to discover a new relation, Christopher."

Christopher crossed the room and went down on his haunches in front of Edwina. She'd been uncharacteristically quiet since he'd appeared, although she'd watched the interactions with wide-eyed attention. "Edwina, do I get a kiss for Christmas Eve?"

To his dismay, she scowled at him. "No, I hate you."

"Edwina!" Harriet gasped.

"He lied to us and pretended to be our friend and he made Annie cry. I heard her in the library before he went in to talk to her. He made us all afraid. I think he's still Wicked Cousin Christopher."

That hurt, mostly because it was all true. "I'm sorry you feel like that," he said in a gentle voice.

The soothing tone failed to achieve its aim. Rage lit Edwina's eyes. "I'm sorry you didn't die in the snow."

"Edwina, that's horrible!" Merry protested. "You little besom!"

The little girl didn't spare her sisters a glance. Instead, she grabbed Jenny and pushed past Christopher to run out of the kitchen.

Harriet stared after her youngest sister in consternation. "I'll go after her and get her to apologize."

Christopher stood, his heart heavy. "No, let her go. She didn't say anything that isn't true. She's been through a trying time. You all have. I'm surprised you two don't hate me as well."

"Edwina loves Christmas," Merry said. "I'm sure she'll settle down by tomorrow."

He admired her optimism. "At least she knows she has a home, whatever she thinks about me."

"You're not angry?" Harriet asked.

He shrugged. "I didn't mean to cause trouble, but without doubt I did. If anyone is angry, it should be you two. You've been deuced generous, giving me the time of day."

"Well said, my lord." Winifred spoke for the first time since his apology. "Now it's time we all sat down and had breakfast. We've had quite enough dramas and upsets for one morning."

"Capital idea," Christopher said, as Anthea came into the kitchen.

"Cousin Christopher has said we can stay," Harriet said, sounding happier than Christopher had ever heard her. "Isn't that wonderful?"

"Wonderful," Anthea said with a shaky smile. Without looking at Christopher, she began to set the table. Despite the smile, she looked worn and downcast. Edwina was right. He'd made Anthea cry, and he ought to be horsewhipped. "That makes the best Christmas present."

"It does," Merry said, heading toward the hallway. "I'll fetch Edwina."

"Thank you, Christopher," Harriet said to him, as she placed a loaf on the table and started to slice it. "However it all started, everything has worked out for the best."

But as he sat at the table and cast a surreptitious glance at a silent Anthea, he couldn't altogether endorse that conclusion.

Anthea came downstairs the next day, feeling as if she attended a funeral instead of the joyous feast that celebrated the Savior's birth. As she approached the drawing room where the family gathered on Christmas morning, she heard laughter and chatter that struck a jarring note with her wretchedness.

Even from behind a closed door, she could tell that her sisters were happy. Or at least Harriet and Merry were. So far, Edwina remained unreconciled to her new cousin. But for Winifred, Harriet, and Merry, knowing that they could continue to live at Yardley had removed an oppressive weight from their spirits.

Each of them had found a chance yesterday to tell Anthea how much they'd dreaded their looming departure from the estate. Anthea had been touched to realize that they'd all done their best to hide their misgivings in order to spare her. She was loved. She knew it, and she should be grateful, instead of stewing on Lord Denton's deceit.

But all she could think about was how he'd lied to her and how he'd lured her into his arms under false pretenses. She'd fretted all night, humiliated that she'd allowed a man of whom she knew nothing to kiss her. Even more mortifying, he'd put his hands on her body.

At least he didn't know that for a brief second yesterday morning, before Parsons turned up, she'd imagined he intended to propose to her. She'd accused him of laughing at her. That would make him split his sides.

How could she have been such a nitwit? How could she imagine herself in love with the scoundrel? He'd said that he wasn't playing her for a fool, but he must be snickering at how close she'd come to surrendering to those skilled caresses. Caresses that she'd been naïve enough to assume meant that he valued her in return.

Still, it was Christmas and she needed to put a brave face on the situation. At least none of her family were about to become homeless. It could be worse.

Although, given how low she felt, that bracing little lecture fell on stony ground.

She pushed open the door and five faces turned in her direction. A small pile of presents sat beside the blazing fire. The scent of greenery tinged the air, and colored paper chains draped from the ceiling.

Anthea deliberately didn't look at the copious amounts of mistletoe adorning every nook and cranny. The last thing that she needed to think about was kissing. She'd spent too much time last night, staring into the darkness with stinging eyes and remembering Lord Denton's lying kisses.

She plastered a smile on her face and hoped it was more convincing than it felt. "Merry Christmas, everyone!"

"Merry Christmas, Annie!" Edwina crouched in the corner with her dolls. To Anthea's relief, she didn't appear to be playing Kill Christopher. She jumped to her feet and ran across the room to fling herself at Anthea.

Anthea crouched down and gave her sister a big hug and a kiss. "How are you this morning?"

"We don't have to leave. I don't need to go to school."

"Indeed you don't." Anthea straightened the red ribbon confining her sister's mop of silky black hair. "You can have as many Christmases at Yardley as you want, sweeting."

"Happy Christmas, Annie," Harriet said, stepping up and smiling down at her.

"And to you, dearest Harry." She rose and hugged the sister who had been such a support over these last difficult months. Harriet's fervent embrace indicated that she, too, was thinking of the reprieve they'd found.

"Happy Christmas, Annie," Merry said, wrapping her arms around both sisters.

"Let me in, too." Edwina pushed her way into the huddle and made everyone laugh.

By the time Anthea untangled herself and crossed to kiss Winifred's cheek, she was blinking away tears. "Happy Christmas, my dear friend."

To her relief, Winifred was willing to let bygones be bygones. Or perhaps she decided that Anthea's unhappiness provided adequate punishment for her sins. "And to you, dear Annie."

Then, because she could put it off no longer, she turned to the last person in the room. "Lord Denton," she said, bobbing a curtsy. "The compliments of the season to you."

She didn't meet his eyes. She feared what he'd see on her face if she did. While such an experienced man must guess that he left her devastated, some scrap of pride refused to hand him that information on a silver salver.

"Why are you curtsying, Annie?" Edwina asked.

"Because he's a nobleman, my love."

"We didn't curtsy, and we call him Christopher."

"You're his cousins. It's different."

"But you're almost his cousin."

"No, I'm not connected to our visitor at all." The heartbreaking truth, as she was well aware.

"I'd like you to call me Christopher, Anthea."

She hated the way that musical baritone made her very bones vibrate with forbidden longing. Because while her mind insisted that he was a mendacious snake, the wanton female that she became in his arms just wanted him to touch her again and never stop.

"You've waited for me with the presents?" Her voice was too high. She caught Harriet's gaze and broadened her smile, until she feared that her cheeks must crack.

"Of course. We always do it together."

"Edwina gives out the gifts," Merry said to Denton.

Everyone found a seat, apart from Edwina, who began to dole out the Christmas presents. Most of the gifts were homemade bits and pieces, although Anthea had saved enough money from housekeeping over the year to buy her sisters some colorful ribbons and Winifred a small cake of scented soap from Shrewsbury.

To her surprise, even Lord Denton received a couple of gifts. Winifred gave him a box of gingerbread, and Harriet had made him a new nightshirt.

"I thought you might like a change from Papa's old shirt," she said.

"It's exquisite, Harry. Thank you."

Anthea had continued not to look at him, but the genuine surprise and gratitude in his voice caught her attention. "Harriet's the best needlewoman of us all." She was thankful that she almost sounded natural.

Merry sidled up to where he sat on the window seat. She held out a small parcel wrapped in tissue paper. "And I made you this."

"Thank you, Merry," he said, accepting the gift and opening it.

Despite this feeling like the worst Christmas of her life, Anthea had to stifle a laugh. Merry wasn't much of an embroiderer. Even from a distance, the two cotton handkerchiefs looked rather tatty.

"I'm sorry they say Lancelot. It was too late to change them to Christopher," Merry said.

Denton caught her around the waist and gave her a kiss on the cheek. "I'll treasure them. I loved being Lancelot in this house."

At last no unopened presents remained, and everyone had exclaimed and admired all the bounty. Winifred stood and smoothed her skirts. "It's time for breakfast, given we can't get out to church this morning. Anthea said she's going to do a Bible reading before lunch to get us square with the Lord on his birthday."

"Wait a minute," Denton said. "You haven't opened my gifts yet."

Confused, Winifred sank back into her chair near the fire. The girls regarded him in equal puzzlement.

"But you didn't know us when you came," Harriet said. "How can you have gifts for us?"

"Magic." When he smiled, Anthea's stomach cramped with yearning.

Why did he have to be so handsome? Given what she now knew about his character, his striking looks shouldn't retain this power over her.

He reached into his inner coat pocket and brought out a handful of folded and sealed papers. "Edwina, I believe you pass out the gifts?"

Edwina approached with a tentative step that made Anthea want to hug her and assure her that everything was all right. "You're not angry with me?"

"No, not at all."

"I said awful things to you yesterday," she mumbled.

He shrugged. "We're family and we love one another. That means we forgive one another, too." Over Edwina's ruffled head, he looked straight at Anthea.

She knew he asked for a sign that she'd pardoned his wrongs against her. Yet how could she, when her heart remained a ragged lump of misery after his betrayal?

"I forgive you, too, then," Edwina said and gave him a quick hug.

"Thank you." He smiled down at her, as if he really did care. "Now give these out please."

Edwina was already a quick reader, so soon all her sisters clutched a letter.

"When did you do this?" Harriet asked without opening hers.

"I couldn't sleep last night, so I came downstairs after midnight. I hoped the Christmas fairy might visit, but sadly I remained alone."

His effrontery had Anthea gasping, but to her relief, everyone else was too intrigued with the unexpected largesse to pay attention.

"Aren't you going to see what the letters say?" she asked through a tight throat.

Harriet was the first to open hers. Anthea watched her sister's expression freeze into disbelief. She looked up and goggled at Lord Denton. "I don't understand."

He smiled at the girl with more of that breathtaking charm that made Anthea's heart squeeze with painful longing. "Of course you do."

"But it's too much."

"It's what you deserve. It means you'll never again worry that you'll lose the roof over your head."

"What is it, Harry?" Merry asked. They could all tell something notable had happened.

Harriet's eyes glittered with tears as she surveyed her sisters. "Cousin Christopher has given me the Yardley estate."

Astonishment held Anthea tongue-tied. It was an act of prodigal generosity.

Before she could question such an extravagant gift, he was speaking. "If you'd been a boy, it would have come to you by right."

"I'm not a boy," Harriet said faintly.

"No," said Merry. "You're an heiress!"

"Precisely," Denton said. "I'll be your trustee until you're twenty-one. I'll send my man of business up here to help you make plans to improve the estate. I'll also fund any projects that we decide are worth pursuing. Once you come of age, you can make your own decisions. However I suspect that you might welcome some advice in the beginning, as you come to terms with being chatelaine of the estate."

"Th...thank you seems so inadequate," Harriet said, looking dazed.

His smile was kind. "It's all I want to hear."

"Then thank you." Harriet stared down at the paper in her hand as if she couldn't yet believe it.

"Aren't you going to open your letters, Merry and Edwina?" he asked.

Merry carefully broke the seal on her letter and took a few seconds to read it, then she raised wondering eyes. "You've settled ten thousand pounds on me."

"Yes. Again, I'll be your trustee and like Harry, you'll receive your inheritance when you're twenty-one or when you marry, if that comes first."

Edwina, who had observed all this with wide eyes, ripped open her letter with considerably less discretion than Merry, then squealed with delight. "I've got ten thousand pounds, too. Thank you, Cousin Christopher."

"My pleasure." He smiled at her. "I can't help feeling I was fated to come here this Christmas to right a grave injustice."

"We're not poor anymore." Merry sounded like she couldn't credit the change in her circumstances. "You've been so terribly kind. We weren't far wrong calling you Lancelot. You're a knight in shining armor, come to our rescue."

The praise left him looking taken aback. "It's what you all deserve. I've discovered a whole new family this Christmas."

Harriet rose and crossed to kiss him on the cheek. "Wicked Cousin Christopher has turned into Father Christmas. How can we repay you?"

"Just use your inheritances wisely."

"I promise I will."

"It's such a relief to know that we don't have to leave Yardley," Merry said. "Isn't it, Anthea?"

Anthea, who had been quiet through all the revelations, smiled at her sister. Inside, she was a mass of confusion. She hated that Lord Denton had lied to her, but his lavish gifts this morning had done so much good to her family. She didn't know where to look or what to do. "I'm so glad."

"While this will always be your home, I want you to lead a life appropriate for gently born young ladies with prospects," Denton said. "I hope you'll come and go a bit more than you have. I'd love to host you all in London next year and show you the sights."

"We can go to Astley's Circus," Harriet said.

"And to the British Museum," Merry added.

"And the Royal Menagerie," Edwina said, as if life offered no greater pleasure.

"And I'll take you down to Surrey to meet my mother and my brother. There are also a lot of relations who will be eager to make your acquaintance. Then when the time comes, I'll sponsor you each for a season in London. My mother will be in alt to take you around to the balls and parties. It's one of the abiding regrets of her life that she only had two rough-and-tumble boys, instead of a couple of daughters to share her interest in fashion."

All three girls stared at him in such wonder that he burst out laughing. "It's all true. You have my word on it."

"I call that very prettily done," Winifred said, smiling at her charges.

Excited chatter filled the room as Harriet, Merry, and Edwina exclaimed over the improvement in their fortunes and questioned Denton about London and the rest of the Trant family. After making a couple of halfhearted comments expressing amazement and pleasure, Anthea took the opportunity to slip out of the room. She was crossing the hall when she heard someone behind her.

"Anthea?" It was Denton, which was no surprise, although she wished to heaven that he hadn't followed her.

She wiped a surreptitious tear from her eye. "Yes?"

"Don't run away."

She turned, trying not to look at him. She knew to her cost that it hurt when she looked at him. "I thought I'd start getting breakfast ready."

"That can wait."

"Yes, it can." She braced her shoulders, preparing to say what she must. This time, she made herself meet his gaze. "That was ridiculously generous."

He shrugged, as if he hadn't transformed so many lives this morning. "It was the right thing to do. I'm a rich man. I don't need the Yardley estate. You and your sisters do. Not to mention that it's your home."

She brushed away another tear. "I can't imagine another man in England who would have done what you did today. I don't know how to thank you. My sisters' future is secure. Winifred has a home into her old age. Harriet will have help to turn the estate into the thriving enterprise it should be."

"You'll have a home, too."

This time, more than one tear fell, which infuriated her. She'd intended to be cool and dignified, but coolness and dignity hovered out of reach. "You must know I can't stay."

He frowned. "What in Hades do you mean?"

"I can't live here as your pensioner. It would make me feel like...you paid me for what happened between us." And seeing him when he married, as surely he must, if only to keep the title going, would break her heart. No, it was better that she left and did her best to forget that she'd ever met him.

He went stark white, and a muscle flickered in his lean cheek. "What the devil nonsense is this? Harriet now owns the manor, and she wants you to stay. So do your other sisters. You're the center of this household. You must know that."

All of this was so painful. It was bad enough suffering an excruciating case of unrequited love, without having to deal with losing her home as well. "Nonetheless I have to go."

His frown of confusion turned into one of displeasure. "Don't let your pride lead you astray, Anthea. If seeing me is such a burden, I promise never to visit."

She shook her head. "The girls would hate that. They're almost as fond of Christopher as they were of Lancelot."

He growled deep in his throat and raked his fingers through his hair. "Yes, they've forgiven me. But they love you. You'll break their hearts if you go."

"Hearts can mend," she said, hoping to glory that it was true. Because right now, hers felt like it split into two tattered halves. "I'll arrange to see them now and again."

He looked angry. Worse, he looked hurt. "Do you hate me so much?"

She bit her lip to smother a protest that she didn't hate him at all. Shaking her head, she turned toward the stairs. She'd been heading toward the kitchen, but this awful scene made her desperate for a few minutes alone in her room. Once she no longer felt like she was about to crack into a million pieces, she'd come back downstairs and pretend this was the best Christmas ever.

"You're a stubborn wench, Anthea Bryars," he said as she trudged away.

"I've had to be stubborn to keep my family together," she said in a thick voice. The tears in her eyes meant that she could hardly see where she was going. She prayed that she didn't stumble or knock anything over. That would be the last straw.

"I'm sure you have. But now your family is safe. You can think about what you want."

I want you.

Despite everything, nothing had changed that. She suspected that it would never change. As he said, she was stubborn and her heart was set on him. Forever, she feared.

"I want a little privacy," she said in a hoarse voice. She wasn't far off breaking down. "At least grant me that."

Anthea reached the base of the staircase and curled her hand around the wrought-iron banister.

He'd see that she was shaking, but then he knew she was crying, so what did it matter?

After a prickling pause, he spoke in an uncompromising tone. "Very well. I can see you're distraught. Run away from me now, but tomorrow we'll talk. I'm not ready to let this go. I'm not ready to let *you* go."

She didn't turn to look at him. "You must see you have to," she said with a hint of grimness.

"All I see is that you're set on riding straight to perdition, and to hell with anybody else."

Her hands clenched hard on the cold metal rail, as she told herself that she could get through this. A bit of heartache wouldn't kill her. Once she left Yardley, she could start to rebuild her life, find a purpose, seek some happiness.

But that could never happen while she remained in contact with Christopher Trant.

CHAPTER TWELVE

$\mathcal{C}$hristopher lay awake most of the night, stewing on damned obstinate women who couldn't see what was good for them, despite the answer being as plain as the nose on their face.

A very pretty nose and a very pretty face.

But that didn't stop him wanting to give Anthea a good talking-to. Followed by a thorough kissing.

He'd always feared that when she realized he'd lied to her, she'd never forgive him. But the reality of her rejection was more painful than his worst imaginings. In fact, it was hell on earth. Regrets at this stage were futile, but he'd give his soul for the chance to start again and tell her the truth from the beginning.

Not long before dawn, he fell into a restless sleep. Now when he checked the pocket watch that he'd fished out of Mistral's saddlebags, he discovered it was close to eleven.

He rolled out of bed and pushed the curtains wide to reveal a stunning view. A bright blue sky. Sparkling snow. And an unfamiliar but rather fine bay horse hitched up beside the front door.

Horror turned his gut to ice. His last hope, already hanging by the narrowest of threads, was about to come crashing down.

Yesterday, he'd intended to have a serious talk to Anthea. But she'd been so heartsick when he accosted her in the hall that he couldn't bear tormenting her further.

She'd come down to breakfast after about half an hour upstairs and had done her best to pretend to enjoy the day's festivities. In all the excitement, her sisters didn't think to confirm Anthea's plans for after Christmas, and he knew that she wouldn't spoil everyone's day by announcing her departure.

Her cheerful act was a travesty. She'd been as brittle as a dry leaf, and the tension around her lovely eyes told him that she had a headache.

He'd thought that nobody else had noticed, but as the day progressed, both Harriet and Winifred had asked if anything was wrong. She'd brushed off their expressions of concern with an artificial laugh.

He'd planned to get her alone after the sumptuous Christmas lunch, planned to mark the family's last Yuletide at Yardley and now celebrating the start of a new era. But Anthea had stuck close to her sisters and hard as he tried, he couldn't lure her away for a quiet word.

He'd hoped to see her after she put Edwina to bed, but she didn't come downstairs again. Although he'd waited in the drawing room until after midnight, long past everyone else retired.

The sensible part of him knew that she'd never again sneak out in the dead of night to kiss him. But he was a man in love. Right now, his sensible self wasn't in charge.

Because he'd failed to get her to himself yesterday, he faced a much greater failure this morning. The sort of failure that left a life in ruins.

Frantic to break up what he feared was taking place downstairs, he flung on his clothes. He didn't bother to shave or comb his hair. He slammed out of his room, sprinted down the corridor and took the stairs two at a time. Once he reached the hall, he hesitated. He was panting for breath, but it was dread that made his heart gallop.

"Good morning, Christopher." Harriet came in from the kitchen with a large pottery jug in her hand. "How are you this morning?"

Devil take it, he had no time for social niceties. He was about to lose everything that he'd ever wanted. He still might, but be buggered if he meant to take his defeat lying down.

"Harry, where's Anthea?" he asked, making no attempt to conceal his agitation.

Harriet frowned. "She's in the library."

He whirled around. "Thanks."

"But she's with Dr. Hobson. You can't go in there. She's—"

Christopher had already gone. He wasn't a man with the habit of praying, but a voice in his mind kept saying, "Don't let me be too late. Don't let me be too late."

He wrenched the door open, expecting to catch Anthea in Hobson's arms.

When she looked up from where she stood alone, staring down into the fire, he crashed to a trembling stop on the threshold.

"Christopher..." she said in astonishment.

He was in too much of a state to pay much attention to the fact that she hadn't called him Lord Denton. Although every time that she'd called him Lord Denton over these last two days, he'd wanted to punch his fist through a window.

His agitated gaze swept the room. "Where's Hobson?"

She looked more startled than ever. He couldn't blame her. He'd barked like a sergeant major addressing a raw recruit. "He's gone."

"I just came from the hall."

Her brow wrinkled in bewilderment. "He went out through the French doors."

Hell. Hell. Hell. Settle down, man.

Christopher knew that he was acting like a lunatic. He sucked in a shuddering breath and struggled to sound like a reasonable human being and not a raving maniac. Yet his voice emerged hoarse with the force of his emotions. "Don't marry him, Anthea."

She stepped back and glanced around the room as if seeking some escape. "I—"

"Marry me instead." He sliced the air with a wild gesture. "Marry me, Anthea. *Marry me.*"

A shaking hand crept up to the base of her neck, as she viewed him with what seemed to be horror. His sinful, longing heart plunged to his boots.

But he wasn't giving up. Not yet. Not ever, if he had any choice in the matter.

Before she could speak and dash his dreams into the dust, he plunged on. "I know he's a better man than I am. Yet however much he loves you, he couldn't love you half as much as I do. Nobody in the world could love you as much as I do."

"You—" she began, looking overwhelmed.

"Don't say no. For the love of God, don't." He dared to step closer. "I've lied to you, and I regret that more than I can say. But I swear I'm not lying now. I'll never lie to you again. For pity's sake, my darling, can't you see that I'm lost without you? Forgive me and marry me, and let me try to convince you to fall in love with me."

Her slender throat moved as she swallowed. "I...I don't think it works like that."

God help him, was he too late? Not just to stop her from marrying another man, but to make her realize that she belonged with him? He couldn't endure it, if that was so.

A premonition of looming failure weighted his words. "Please, Anthea, please give me another chance. Don't marry Hobson."

"I...I'm not going to marry him. I just told him that. That's why he went out the back way. He was more...disappointed than I expected he would be."

Christopher hadn't taken a full breath since he'd woken to see Hobson's horse outside. Now, he managed to inhale, and some of the red mist evaporated from his mind.

For the first time since he'd burst in, he paused to take stock of his surroundings. Upon a closer look, Anthea didn't look wildly happy. In fact, she appeared strained and tired. And she'd just said that she hadn't accepted the clodhopper's proposal. Or had he imagined that?

"I'm not surprised," Christopher said, at last sounding half-sane. "You're a prize, and he knows it."

Anthea's hands twined at her waist, as she regarded him with an uncertain expression. "When I said I was going away, I didn't mean that I was going to marry Philip. I never wanted to marry him. I told you that. I thought that I might have to, to save the girls from Great-Aunt Dorcas. Your Christmas gifts to my sisters let me send him away with a clear conscience. Now I can seek a position as a governess, without worrying about making a home for my sisters and Winifred."

Christopher struggled to make sense of what she said. One thing was blightingly, cursedly clear. It was difficult to speak past the jagged boulder of anguish in his throat. "You'd rather be a governess than my wife?"

A dismissive huff escaped her. "Until now, I didn't know becoming your wife was one of my options."

With every second, his madness receded. He frowned, as he considered what she said with a modicum of logic. That almost sounded as if he might have a chance. He didn't realize that he'd moved, but he seemed to be holding her hand.

"Now that you know, what do you say?" He repeated the words that he'd never said to another woman. This time, he didn't shout, but spoke with a throbbing intensity that mirrored the depth of his emotion. "Anthea, I love you more than I can say. That was why I couldn't bear to admit I was Wicked Cousin Christopher. I couldn't take the risk of you hating me. I knew you were the one for me from the moment I first saw you."

"That can't be true." Her confused expression didn't encourage optimism, although at least she wasn't trying to get him to release her hand. "The first time you saw me, you snapped my head off."

Christopher responded with a wry grunt of laughter. His hopes, dashed a few seconds ago, began to sprout like spring growth. She hadn't said no yet. "I knew, even when I was lying in the snow half out of my head. I've been out of my head over you ever since. Please say that you'll think about becoming my wife, Anthea. I can't live without you."

"Oh, I've already thought about that." To his surprise, she smiled. All of a sudden, she didn't look half so downhearted as she had when he blundered in. "I'd much rather marry you than take on responsibility for another woman's children."

His heart gave a great thud of triumph, then another. His grip on her hand firmed. By heaven, he meant to hold onto her forever. "Did you just agree to have me, you magnificent woman?"

Her smile widened. When he'd broken into the room, she'd looked disconsolate and defeated. Now she looked like she could take possession of the whole world and wear it as a pearl around her neck. "I believe I did."

He swept her into his arms and kissed her with all the relief and gratitude and adoration in his heart. He wasn't on the verge of losing her. She'd promised to be his. Anthea Bryars would become the Countess of Denton, and he couldn't be more elated.

To his surprise, she kissed him back with a desperate fervor that sparked immediate passion. She wrapped her arms around him and pressed close, as though she couldn't bear anything to separate them.

Breathless, he raised his head and stared down into her flushed face. "Anthea, I'm going to make you the happiest woman in England."

Shining eyes devoured him, as if she couldn't get enough of him. "I am the happiest woman in England. I thought I'd never see you again."

He was confident enough now to answer that with a derisive grunt. "As if I'd let you get away. I'm no fool. I know what a treasure I've found. Although I must admit to a few excruciating minutes when I feared that you'd accepted Hobson's proposal."

She laid her hand on his cheek, then jerked it away with a gasp of surprise. "You're all bristly."

"I didn't even comb my hair before I rushed down to rip you from his arms."

She laughed at that, before her expression turned serious. "Silly man. How can I marry someone else when I'm so terribly in love with you?"

"Wait." Stunned, he stared into her beautiful face. "You love me?"

"So very, very much." She rose on her toes and kissed him quickly. "When I thought you were playing spiteful games with me, it broke my heart."

His lips curved into a beatific smile. "I was never playing with you. It was because everything was so important that I made such a God-awful mess of it all. Tell me you forgive me. After fearing that you'd loathe me until the day you died, I need to hear it in words of one syllable so I can be sure. My brain has been in chaos since the day I met you."

"You have had a bump on the head."

Christopher thought he'd never again see that teasing glint in her eyes. He almost didn't mind that she left him in suspense over whether he'd heard her right, when she said she loved him. "I've had a blow to the heart, more like. I'm sorry I pretended to be Lancelot. I hope you're content to end up with Christopher instead."

Her hand moved against his face in a caress so loving that his blood turned to sugar. "Watching Christopher single-handedly create a secure future for my sisters was enough to make me fall in love with him all over again. How can I thank you for that?"

"You can say that you'll marry me as soon as we call the banns. I fancy a winter wedding in Shropshire." His smile returned and a measure of his self-assurance, which had taken a thrashing over the last few days. "What do you say?"

Anthea loved him. She was willing to overlook his sins against her. She said she'd marry him. Altogether he'd call that a mighty fine result.

She responded with a choked laugh, although her eyes told him that any urge to cry stemmed from overwhelming joy. "I say that's a capital idea, my dear, *dear* Lord Denton."

This Christmas had delivered a miraculous gift. He'd be grateful for the rest of his life. Christopher gathered Anthea close and kissed her with every ounce of the invincible love that filled his heart.

CHAPTER THIRTEEN

Late January, 1819

The best suite of rooms in Shrewsbury's best inn left Anthea wide-eyed with wonder. She wasn't yet used to being a countess. Good heavens, she wasn't yet used to being a bride. And now she was married and waiting for her dashing new husband to come to her. Almost exploding with anticipation, she sat up in the elaborate fourposter bed that was more ornate than anything at Yardley.

She wore a beautiful and shockingly revealing nightdress that Harriet had sewn and given to her today before she wed Lord Denton in the village church. Her hair hung heavy and loose around her shoulders and under what felt like a mere drift of silk, she was naked.

The luxurious room was decorated with masses of hothouse flowers, a gift from the Earl of Halston and his beautiful wife Stella, who had extensive greenhouses on their estate Prestwick Place. Candelabra lit everything to gold. A fire crackled in the grate. A tray of decanters and delicacies was set out on a carved chest that looked like it came from a palace. The heavy curtains were drawn against another snowy night, although it had been a perfect winter's day, cold and clear and sunny.

A perfect day altogether. Full of love and laughter, and good wishes for the happy couple. The church had been packed with a mixture of locals and Christopher's family and smart London friends.

If Anthea hadn't been so alight with happiness, she might have been daunted. But having married the man she loved so much, she sailed through meeting so many members of the beau monde, including Christopher's cousins, the Halstons, and his friends, Lord and Lady Colville. She'd already established a warm relationship with Christopher's mother and brother, who had spent the last fortnight at Yardley.

In fact, the house had been heaving with visitors since she and Christopher got engaged, including what felt like a battalion of solicitors who worked on finalizing the various legal settlements. Harriet was now the owner of Yardley. Merry and Edwina were officially heiresses. Anthea herself was well provided for as the new Countess of Denton.

In the month since his proposal, she and Christopher had had difficulty finding a private moment together. The terrible weather hadn't helped. They'd been confined to a modest manor house, packed with curious young girls, a watchful Winifred, and his mother and brother, who seemed to have arrived with half a household of servants. Not to mention a London modiste and her assistants, who had been hard at work creating an extravagant wardrobe, not just for the bride, but for her sisters. Even Winifred found herself in possession of half a dozen stylish new outfits.

Most beautiful of all Anthea's new dresses was the cream velvet wedding gown that she'd worn, walking down the aisle in the company of her sisters as bridesmaids. She'd felt like a princess. When Christopher turned to watch her, his eyes glowing with unabashed love and pride, she'd graduated from feeling like a princess to feeling like a queen.

They'd left Yardley in the late afternoon in a luxurious carriage, which had carried them the ten miles to Shrewsbury with barely a bump. Christopher had taken advantage of getting her to himself at last to kiss her with a thoroughness that had made her head swim.

It was the longest time they'd spent without interruption since the day that she'd agreed to marry him. Passion had blazed hot and fast and left her in a lather of sensual excitement about what was to happen between them in this bed tonight.

Since then, they'd settled in at the inn and eaten an excellent and very early dinner. After that, her new maid had readied her for her wedding night. Anthea wasn't used to a servant dedicated to her needs, and there had been something almost sybaritic in having help to bathe and dress and prepare for her bridegroom.

The door from the next room opened, and Christopher strode into the chamber, only to stop as suddenly as if he'd crashed into a pane of glass. "My God, darling, you're a vision."

"I should hope so." Anthea smiled at him, just so happy that after all their misunderstandings and quarrels, they'd reached this point in the end. "That girl brushed and polished and anointed me until I feel like a sacrificial lamb."

Christopher laughed. "I'm going to increase her wages. You were a ravishing bride, but right now, you take my breath away."

"Thank you. You're rather appealing yourself."

He glanced down at the black and gold dressing gown covering the long, lean body that had stirred her curiosity from the first. "I'm pleased you think so."

"I feel like I've hardly seen you over the last four weeks. I keep waiting for someone to interrupt us."

Another chuckle. "We've had more chaperones since we got engaged than we had before. When I already felt like we had more than enough supervision. It's a good thing I'm so dashed fond of my cousins, or I swear I'd have tossed at least one of them out the window. Every time I thought I had you to myself, Harriet or Merry or Edwina would appear."

Anthea giggled. "Or Winifred."

"Or Winifred in her winsome nightcap." He scanned the room. "Are you sure she's not hiding behind the curtains?"

"Check if you like."

She laughed, as he crossed to fling back the green velvet to reveal a mullioned window but no ageing governess. He turned to her, eyes alight with amusement and what she'd learned to read as sexual interest.

The carriage ride from Yardley had been over far too soon. Now an entire night stretched ahead. Tomorrow they traveled to a manor on the rugged Welsh coast, where they'd honeymoon for a blissful fortnight. Anthea suspected that the place would be cold and windy, but that only gave her an excuse to stay inside with her delectable husband.

He gestured toward the tray. "Would you like a glass of wine?"

She shook her head. "No, thank you."

"Would you like something to eat?"

"No."

He cocked one dark eyebrow at her. "So what would you like?"

He knew what she wanted, the scoundrel. She'd desired him from the beginning, when she'd sneaked back to catch a glimpse of his naked body the night that she rescued him. Since discovering that he loved her as much as she loved him, she hadn't hidden her eagerness to learn the secrets of the marital act.

"That's easy. I'd like you to kiss me."

That eyebrow angled higher. "Just kiss you?"

She released a long exhalation. "And the rest."

"You're not afraid?" This time, he wasn't teasing.

She shrugged. "I'm a little nervous. That's natural. But I'm sure you know what you're doing, and we've got time to get this right if need be."

That made him laugh. "Practice makes perfect? You know what's going to happen?"

"My mother told me. She didn't believe women should be ignorant about something with such a bearing on their lives."

"Good for her."

"She said it's wonderful with the right man. Given she had two happy marriages, I'm guessing she spoke with some authority."

"I believe it can hurt the first time," he said, his smile fading. "You might have something else to forgive me for tomorrow."

Anthea stared across the room at him and struggled to express something that had lodged in her mind over these last weeks. "Actually, I'm rather grateful that I did get to know you as Lancelot rather than Lord Denton. It meant by the time I discovered that you were Wicked Cousin Christopher, I was already head over heels in love with you. I was past the point of putting up any real resistance."

She watched a shadow fade from his expression. A shadow that until now, she hadn't realized was there.

He sucked in a deep breath, and his shoulders relaxed. "You really have forgiven me?"

She'd told him that she had, but she now recognized that he hadn't believed her. Or not entirely.

He believed her now.

"With all my heart. Just as I love you with all my heart." She extended her hand toward him. "Come to me, Christopher. Come to me, my love. I've hungered for you for an age. Don't make me wait any longer."

"My darling…" He flung off the dressing gown and crossed the room in a couple of paces. She had a brief impression of long muscled limbs and a broad naked chest before he kneeled on the bed and swept her up into his arms.

His mouth was hot and voracious, as his kisses sent her whirling out into a new and dazzling universe. For the first time, they needn't fear anyone stopping them. These kisses were a forerunner to the ultimate mystery of his body moving inside hers. Soon, he'd make her his wife in fact as well as by law. The thought sent a primitive thrill rocketing through her.

He drew away long enough to pull the delicate nightdress over her rumpled head. Before she had a chance to think of covering her nakedness, he buried his hands in her hair and hauled her up for more mind-spinning kisses. Kisses that after an eternity of pleasure shifted to cover her shoulders and breasts.

With great care, he lowered her onto her back and came down over her, their legs tangling as he stretched out. She cried out when he took the aching peak of her breast between his lips and applied pressure so exquisite that surely she must die of delight.

His hand squeezed her other breast, then stroked her into a squirming agony of longing that had her writhing against the sheets in demand for more.

Anthea moaned and sighed and gasped for breath, as he used teeth and tongue and lips to arouse her. All the while his hands smoothed across her skin, pausing to discover and tantalize, until he ventured between her legs to explore the hidden folds of her sex.

She cried out again at the bolt of blinding sensation sizzling through her. Her nails dug into the skin of his back as he touched her again and again, building that extraordinary pleasure.

"Don't stop." She didn't recognize the husky voice as hers.

With his lips devouring hers, she felt a subtle stretching in her most private place. He penetrated her with one finger, while his thumb tormented the source of those searing surges. The throb between her legs turned liquid, as he moved his finger in and out, establishing an intoxicating rhythm that had her begging for more.

Instinct made her part her legs wider and lift her knees on either side of his narrow hips. When she arched, his hand slid away from her cleft.

The pressure that she felt next was more insistent. She curled her fingers around his taut shoulders, gripping tight as he pushed inside her.

"Can you bear it?" Christopher asked in a constricted voice, rising on his elbows to stare down into her face.

"Yes," she said, as her body stretched to accommodate him. It was uncomfortable but not intolerable. "I want to be yours. Forever. I love you."

"And I love you, Anthea."

Christopher kissed her again, and she bowed up to take him deeper. Groaning against her lips, he pushed forward. She released a muffled protest, as red-hot pain streaked through her. Then her body received his, and that second of searing pain was forgotten.

This time, his groan was long and guttural and expressed vast satisfaction. He broke the kiss and buried his face in the tangle of her hair with an incoherent growl of masculine appreciation.

For a pulsating interval, Anthea lay beneath him, adjusting to the physical invasion. He filled her in a way that banished the memory of her lonely years at Yardley. She and her husband were joined now and for the rest of their lives. Her frantic clasp on his shoulders relaxed as she eased around him, accepting him into her body and accepting him as the other half of her soul.

When he started to move, she was ready to embark on the journey to paradise. She'd already found pleasure in his arms. When he'd kissed her, and tonight when he explored her body. Now the powerful reaction that built inside her as he began a steady thrust and withdrawal astounded her. He transported her beyond the bounds of earth, as the promise of heaven coiled tighter and tighter inside her.

Then Christopher seemed to go deeper than before to reach a part of her that exploded into fiery glory. She called out his name in a choked exclamation, before her body spasmed into incandescent light.

Through her convulsions, she was aware of his movements becoming wilder. His breath sawed in erratic gusts. On an audible exhalation, every muscle in his body tightened. Heat spurted into her womb, as he lost himself inside her.

For a transcendent interval, she lay beneath the man she loved, reveling in his passionate possession. The charged, astonishing peak ebbed away in gradual waves that made her feel as if she drifted back to earth like a feather dropped from the clouds.

After a long, gasping embrace, he rolled to the side, taking her with him. He kissed her with a weary gratitude that filled her with poignant emotion.

"I love you, Anthea," he said gruffly, wrapping his arms about her.

"I love you, Christopher," she said in return, nestling into his side as her titanic reaction faded to radiant pleasure.

She might have fallen asleep for a minute or two. It had been a long and busy day, and that earth-shaking encounter just now had wrung every drop of response from her.

When she opened her eyes, Christopher leaned against the pile of pillows and she was curled up against his chest. She drew a deep breath, noting the tang of sexual satisfaction in the air, as well as the heady fragrance of Lord Halston's flowers. Christopher stroked her hair with a tenderness that made her heart swell with adoration.

She turned and placed a gentle kiss just above his nipple. "My mother was right. It is marvelous with the right man."

His hold tightened "I hurt you."

"A little. At first. But after that... Oh, my stars, Christopher, how wonderful it all was. How wonderful that we can do it again and again."

A low chuckle rumbled in her ear, as he gave a hank of her hair a soft tug. "I promised to worship you with my body, you'll recall."

She lifted her head and gave him a long kiss that conveyed passion, but also how much she loved him. Before the kiss could catch fire, she drew away. "I feel worshipped."

This time, he kissed her. "I do worship you. You're everything to me, Anthea."

She peered into his brilliant golden eyes and saw unshakeable love. And, yes, a light that looked like reverence, however unworthy she might be. "You make me so happy."

The charming, rakish smile that never failed to set her wayward pulses racing curled his lips and transformed him into the soul of devilry. "Then let me make you happy all over again, my dearest wife."

When she responded with a breathless giggle, he tugged her under him once more and proceeded to kiss her into rapturous confusion.

EPILOGUE

Lorimer Square, Mayfair, 23rd December 1823

On a bleak London afternoon, it might be cold and wet outside. But inside luxurious Trant House, all was warmth and contentment. And anticipation.

Because Harriet, Merry, and Edwina were on their way down from Shropshire to spend Christmas with Anthea and Christopher.

Christopher surveyed his cozy drawing room with its blazing fire and elegant fittings and couldn't help feeling like a lucky man. Not least because of the people in this room, the people he loved best in the world.

Although his three Shropshire cousins held a special place in his heart, too. He hadn't seen them since Easter, so he was eager for their arrival.

"Any sign?" Anthea asked Simon, their rambunctious four-year-old son, who was glued to the window overlooking the square so he would be the first to see the visitors.

"No, not yet," he said without turning around. "I think they've got lost."

Anthea rolled her eyes at Christopher, which made him stifle a laugh. She was sitting at the elegant mahogany desk in the corner, writing a letter. Christopher was in the large leather armchair in front of the hearth, reading the *Times*. Their daughter Ida, almost three, was playing with her blocks on the rug at his feet.

Behind her, a flat padded basket held a one-eared tabby cat and six nursing kittens. Anthea hadn't lost her penchant for rescuing lost and injured animals. Meadowbank was turning into a blasted menagerie, which delighted the children. His gamekeepers had been reassigned to new positions, because hunting was now outlawed on Trant land.

"They said they'd be here before dinner, darling," Anthea said to her restless son. "It could be hours yet. Not to mention it's raining, so they may be held up with the weather."

Simon's groan indicated his poor opinion of his mother's remarks. Their son was bright and energetic and spirited, which wasn't always a blessing. Patience was a virtue he was yet to learn. He was also the image of his mother, with golden hair and blue eyes, and Christopher couldn't be prouder of him. "But they'll be in a hurry to see us."

"Yes, they will be." Simon's aunts, who weren't that much older than he was, doted on him.

Ida looked up from her game. She was a quieter, dreamier child who had inherited Christopher's dark coloring. "Will Wina take me to the park?"

"I'm sure she will," Christopher said, folding up his newspaper and smiling at his daughter. She had his heart on a string and even at two and a half, she knew it. "And if she doesn't, I will."

"Good," she said, going back to piling wooden blocks on top of one another.

"They'll bring us presents," Simon said with such greedy relish that Anthea laughed.

"Yes, no doubt they will, you mercenary little monster."

That made him turn away from the window in confusion. "What's a mersney?"

"A boy who likes to get presents," Christopher said.

Simon shrugged. "It's Christmas. We're supposed to get presents."

"Grandmamma's presents are the best," Ida said, as if there could be no argument about that. The blocks had been a gift from the Dowager Countess, and they'd been a great success. Unlike her Aunt Edwina, Ida so far didn't show much interest in dolls.

"Grandmamma is coming tomorrow. So is Uncle David," Simon said with a hint of self-importance. He liked to lord it over Ida and got frustrated when most of the time, she paid no heed to his pretensions.

As was the case now. Ida had retreated to whatever was going on in her imagination, so her brother's superior comment passed her by.

Christopher hadn't given having children much thought, until his first Christmas in Shropshire when he'd fallen in love with his wife. It was a surprise quite how interesting it proved to observe their personalities develop, often in unexpected ways. Simon and Ida were already little people in their own right. So different from each other, they made a fascinating contrast.

Quiet descended once again, as Simon returned to his vigil and Anthea lowered her head over her correspondence. Instead of picking up the paper, Christopher paused a moment to contemplate his family and think back over almost five years of marriage.

The memories were all happy. He had so many reasons to bless Mistral's stumble in the snowy woods on that afternoon when Anthea had rescued him from freezing to death.

Because she'd rescued him not just from a cold and lonely demise. She'd rescued him from a cold and lonely life.

He'd adored her when he married her, so it surprised him that he only came to love her more each day. He'd always admired her beauty and her courage and her intelligence. Now he added to that list of qualities her steadfastness and perceptiveness and kindness. She'd made his life complete, even before she gave him these two precious, exceptional children. Every day, he thanked his Maker for the gift of this remarkable woman.

As if she knew what he was thinking – that happened often enough not to be an accident, he'd long ago recognized – she lifted her head and gave him a smile. "You're looking rather contemplative."

"I'm thinking that it was a damned good thing that Wicked Cousin Christopher nearly broke his neck on your doorstep five years ago."

She arched her eyebrows as humor lit her eyes. "Oh, nobody's called you Wicked Cousin Christopher in a donkey's age. Even Edwina hasn't played Kill Christopher since you made her an heiress."

He laughed. In the last years, they'd shared plenty of love and oceans of desire, but there had also been laughter. The soul-restoring, life-affirming kind that made a man want to get up in the morning. Or stay in bed and tempt his luscious wife into taking another trip to heaven in his arms.

Yes, they'd been good years. Anthea had soon found her place in society as the Countess of Denton, and she'd become close friends with Stella and with Lord Colville's wife Verena. The beau monde had started calling them the Three Graces.

Christopher and his wife had established a busy, fulfilling life, traveling between London and Shropshire and the family seat at Meadowbank. His cousins were thriving, and he looked forward to watching Harriet take the ton by storm in a couple of months when she arrived in Town for her first season.

"Even Winifred seems to like me these days," he said in a considering tone.

That prompted a huff of amusement from Anthea. "Since she married John, Winifred likes everyone."

To universal surprise but most of all to hers, Winifred had fallen in love with the solicitor Christopher had hired to take over Yardley Hall's affairs. His usual man of business had been occupied with his current work on the Trant properties, so he'd arranged for a partner to replace Uncle Basil's ineffectual lawyer.

John Bateman turned out to be a canny widower, who had straightaway recognized Winifred as the perfect wife for a sober gentleman of substantial means. After a year of sedate wooing, Winifred had relinquished a lifetime of dedicated spinsterhood. She was now a loving stepmother to John's four children and step-grandmother to his dozen grandchildren. She'd also been able to offer her sister a home much more comfortable than her rundown terrace in Manchester.

Because of Winifred's departure for London, Christopher and Anthea had ended up spending a good deal of time at Yardley, keeping an eye on his cousins. But these days, the hall boasted a governess and a tutor and a steward, not to mention a household full of servants. The girls also spent extended periods living with Christopher and Anthea in Mayfair and Surrey. This eight-month gap between visits was unusual.

Simon gave an excited shout and darted toward the door. "They're here!"

With her characteristic calmness, Ida set the last block in place and stood up on her chubby legs.

"Would you like me to carry you, sweetheart?" Christopher asked.

She responded with an emphatic shake of her head. Ida was an independent soul and preferred to manage for herself. "I can do it."

Simon dragged the door open and dashed outside. Ida followed more slowly, leaving Christopher and Anthea alone.

His beautiful wife cast him a rueful look. "That's the end of our quiet life for the next month."

He crossed and took her hand as she rose. "Who wants a quiet life?"

"Not me." Her fingers curled around his in immediate welcome. "Christmas should always be full of joy and noise and games and silliness."

He scanned the opulent room. A wagonload of greenery had arrived from Meadowbank a few days ago, so the whole house was bedecked for the season. "And mistletoe."

"We carry mistletoe in our hearts," she said with another laugh.

"Does that mean I can kiss you whenever I feel like it?"

She sent him a mocking glance, and a smile hovered about her lips. "You do that anyway."

It was true. He couldn't get enough of her, even now when they were a settled married couple with a pair of lovely children. She just needed to blink at him, and he was ready to whisk her away for some stolen delight. Anthea had always been lovely, but these days, she glowed with the sensual air of a woman who desired and who was desired in return.

"All the same, kiss me now before the invasion starts."

Without hesitation, she turned into his arms and kissed him with the sweet enthusiasm that always made his heart pound. "I love you, my darling husband."

"And I love you," he murmured back.

The hubbub of arrival rose from the hall below, as he kissed Anthea again in a silent promise of eternal devotion. Then he curled his arm around her waist and they went downstairs to greet their family.

ABOUT THE AUTHOR

Australian Anna Campbell has written 11 multi award-winning historical romances for Avon HarperCollins and Grand Central Publishing. As an independently published author, she's released more than 30 bestselling stories. Right now, she is working on a new series called Scoundrels of Mayfair, set amidst the glamour and sensuality of Regency London. Anna has won numerous awards for her stories, including RT Book Reviews Reviewers Choice, the Booksellers Best, the Golden Quill (three times), the Heart of Excellence (twice), the Write Touch, the Aspen Gold (twice), and the Australian Romance Readers' favorite historical romance (five times).

Anna loves to hear from her readers. You can find her at:

Website: www.annacampbell.com

facebook.com/AnnaCampbellFans

twitter.comAnnaCampbellOz

bookbub.com/authors/anna-campbell

One Wicked Wish:
A Scandal in Mayfair Book 1

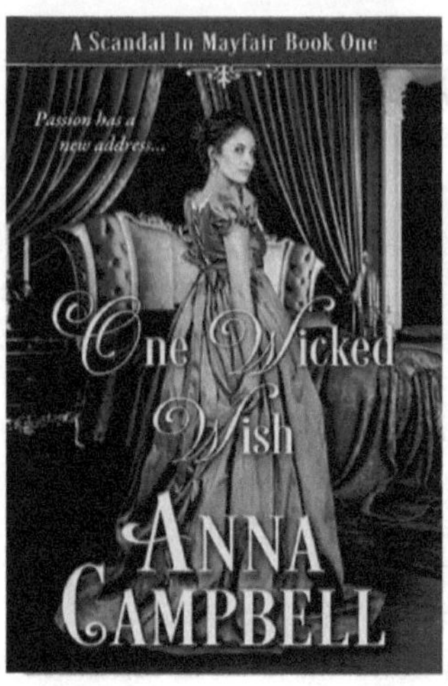

Her secret lover...

Stella Faulkner has been a despised poor relation in her odious uncle's house since she was forced to flee Italy ahead of Napoleon's invasion. In return for a roof over her head, she acts as her cousin's unpaid governess and companion. Stella knows that if she shows the slightest trace of her disgraced mother's wildness, she'll be cast out to face destitution. But after ten years of thankless servitude, Stella encounters a dashing libertine who turns her world to flame. Handsome Lord Halston is irresistible, but every kiss, every caress carries the risk of discovery, and with discovery, disaster.

The rake beguiled...

Grayson Maddox, Earl of Halston, glories in his reputation for charm, seduction, and ruthlessness. His mistresses know that the profligate lord offers them pleasure and luxury, but when he says goodbye, the affair is over. To Halston, love is a sentimental myth and fidelity a trap. One night at a glittering ball, he sees a beautiful woman trying to fade into the crowd of dowdy chaperones and every instinct clamors to make this mysterious lady his. But all bets are off when Stella Faulkner promises to become the lover he'll never forget.

Forbidden passion.

Halston and Stella start a sizzling affair under the cover of a respectable house party at his country estate. But once this interval of heady delight comes to an end, what will become of the humble governess and the wicked earl? Must they return to being strangers as they originally arranged, or will five days of intoxicating sin turn into forever?

Two Secret Sins:
A Scandal in Mayfair Book 2

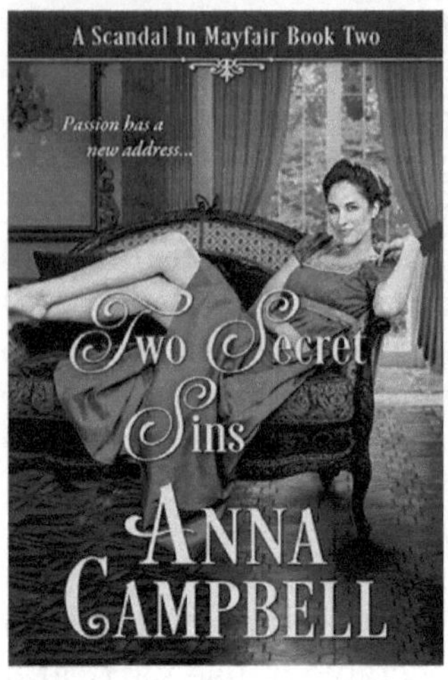

The Saint and the Sinner!

Eliot Ridley, Viscount Colville, is a man of immaculate character with lifelong ambitions to make his mark in parliament. Lady Verena Gerard is a headstrong, independent widow with a string of lovers in her scandalous past. Two people with absolutely nothing in common, apart from the irresistible desire that draws them into an explosive, secret affair.

Now Eliot is so determined to claim the reckless beauty as his own that he's ready to throw away his stainless reputation and his political hopes. What choice does Verena have when he proposes but to end the liaison? Taking a notorious woman as his wife will taint Eliot and his family, not to mention that after the brutal misery of her first marriage, she's vowed never to wed again.

Never say never.

In the glamorous, sophisticated world Eliot and Verena inhabit, wickedness thrives behind closed doors and the only unforgivable sin is falling in love. Will the handsome viscount defy society and Verena's fears to win the bride he wants? Or will Eliot and his wild lady part to follow their separate destinies and forever spurn the forbidden longing in their hearts?

Three Times Tempted:
A Scandal in Mayfair Book 3

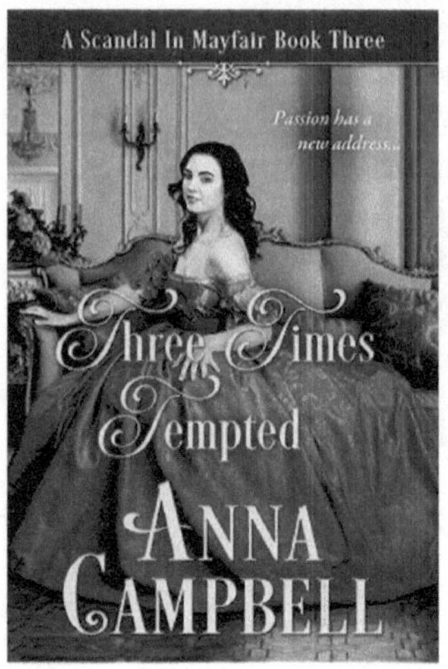

A secret rebel...

Beautiful, spirited Lady Imogen Ridley is the toast of London's glamorous season. Her blue-blooded admirers would be shocked to know that beneath her glittering veneer, she loathes society's shallow snobberies. All she wants is to return to her gardening projects in the country.

Her reckless attempt to spark a scandal that will result in a quick trip home goes awry when she meets a handsome stranger in a dark gazebo. A string of forbidden trysts follow that fateful encounter, as immediate attraction soon turns to blazing passion. But Imogen has been promised to another, and her father is powerful and ruthless. He won't tolerate any challenge to his ambitions for his daughter.

A man from a different world…

American Caleb Black finds himself at odds with England's hidebound rules. Despite his wealth and brilliance as a landscape designer, he's considered little better than a servant in status-obsessed Mayfair. So when he sets his sights on marrying the Earl of Deerforth's lovely daughter, he knows he's asking for trouble.

And trouble is exactly what he gets. Caleb needs to call on all his cleverness and determination to court his exquisite lady, let alone engineer a chance to make her his. With every secret meeting, every stolen caress, desire burns hotter, while danger and disgrace loom ever closer. Will this impossible love affair shatter the towering barriers of class and pedigree? Or will noble lineage, family duty, and centuries of tradition forever separate this man of the people from his aristocratic beloved?

Four Christmas Kisses:
A Scandal in Mayfair Book 4

A mysterious guest at Christmas.

Spirited Anthea Bryars already has enough problems to deal with when a few days before Christmas, she stumbles across an unconscious stranger in the woods. She and her half-sisters will be homeless after New Year, now that Lord Denton has inherited Yardley Hall and given the family their marching orders. The last thing Anthea needs is a handsome, smart-mouthed distraction who makes her long for forbidden pleasures.

Secrets and passion...

After rakish Christopher Trant, Earl of Denton, tumbles from his horse in a snowstorm, his rescuer is the loveliest woman he's ever seen. But waking up the next morning, he's horrified to discover that at Yardley Hall, he's universally hated as Wicked

Cousin Christopher. He'd left London assuming the remote manor house was empty, but it turns out it's occupied by three unknown cousins and an alluring lady called Anthea. To play for time, he pretends that his injuries have stolen his memory. But one small lie leads to others, until he's so tangled in desire and deception, he doesn't know where to turn.

A season of goodwill?

Will the revelation of Christopher's identity destroy all his chances to win Anthea? Or might the magic of Christmas unite these two unlikely lovers and conjure up a bright new future for the whole family? Could four Christmas kisses mean goodbye or happy forever after?

www.ingramcontent.com/pod-product-compliance
Lightning Source LLC
Chambersburg PA
CBHW030758190726
48285CB00003B/916